a DOG and his GIRL
MYSTERIES

3

Cry
WOOF

Don't miss any of Dodge and Cassie's adventures!

Play Dead
Dead Man's Best Friend

a DOG and his GIRL MYSTERIES

3

Cry WOOF

Jane B. Mason

and Sarah Hines Stephens

SCHOLASTIC INC.

ISBN 978-0-545-43626-7

12 11 10 9 8 7 6 5 4 3 2 1   13 14 15 16 17 18/0

Printed in the U.S.A.   40
First printing, October 2013

The text type was set in Adobe Garamond Pro.
Book design by Elizabeth B. Parisi

CHAPTER 1

The doors to the Bellport Police Station whooshed open, and Dodge and I stepped inside. "Hey, guys," Deb Brubaker, the dark-haired dispatcher, greeted from behind her desk. "What's doing?"

Dodge let out a little bark in response — a friendly hello — and I reached down to give him a pat.

"We just thought we'd drop by, say hi to Mom," I replied with a shrug, even though that wasn't *exactly* true. Dodge and I didn't ever just "drop by," especially at the station. We were detectives — always alert, always looking for clues, always sniffing out information. Especially Dodge. My ninety-pound German shepherd had a nose for trouble, and could sniff out anything.

Deb nodded and we moved into the big open room with the cubicles, heading for Mom's office. Mom was chief of the Bellport police force, the boss of everyone in the station. She used to be Dodge's boss, too, before he lost his job. My partner wasn't just any dog — he was a trained K-9. He'd served on the Bellport force for several years, and his first partner was one of the best cops in the unit, my uncle Mark. But about a year ago a deadly on-the-job explosion killed my uncle. He was gone, just like that. And so was half of Dodge's hearing, and his job. My poor pooch went from the top of the heap to the bottom — partnerless, homeless, jobless. *Ka-boom!* The only silver lining was that those nightmarish events led Dodge to me.

When we lost Uncle Mark, my whole family sort of fell apart. Nobody knew what to do or how to be. Then Dodge came to live with us, and little by little, we got better. We kept going. I can't speak for every Sullivan, but Dodge *definitely* saved me. When he moved in he gave me a reason to get up in the morning. He gave me his friendship. His trust. His loyalty. His love. Not to mention the fact that he seriously improved my detective skills.

Just remembering losing Uncle Mark was awful, and made my hand automatically drop into Dodge's fur for comfort. Sensing that my thoughts were wandering (reading my mind was a thing he just did), Dodge nosed my palm. I knew what he was thinking, too — time to get sleuthing. He led the way to Mom's office door.

Before we set foot inside the office, we knew two things: Mom was at her desk, and she was talking to someone. A look around the edge of the door revealed that she was on the phone. But the question remained — who was she talking to?

Mom raised a finger to let us know she saw us and needed a minute. Dodge crossed to the desk for a scratch while I pretended to be interested in the awards on the wall. I glanced back at Mom. She held the receiver away from her ear for a moment and gave it a look that spoke volumes. She had that "I'm too busy for this" expression — the person on the other end was wasting her time. I knew that expression all too well. Mom always had a ton to do, at home and at work. Being chief was a really big job.

I didn't mind that Mom was busy; it gave me a chance to poke around. There were always interesting things to find in the police chief's office. After I "examined" the walls — there was a new picture of Mom posing with a class of third graders — I moved on to the desk. It was piled high with work. It looked messy, but knowing Mom, there was a system. A stack of newspapers teetering on the corner caught my eye and I scanned some headlines. There wasn't much of interest, just some mundane articles about gas prices, an upcoming election, and — oh! the sentencing of former Mayor Baudry — the result of our most recently cracked case! Dodge's snout sniffed the edge of the newspaper and I ruffled his ears. He couldn't read, of course. But sometimes it seemed like he could sniff essential information right off a page.

"Yes, Madame," Mom said in her patient voice. I could hear the sigh behind it. "Yes, I'm sure that was alarming for you."

I half smiled and half grimaced as I realized that she was talking to Madame LeFarge. Mom said that every town had a crazy cat lady, and Madame LeFarge was ours. Madame called the station almost daily, bothering the officers with silly complaints and paranoid ideas. She was absolutely certain that everyone in Bellport was against her. Totally untrue, of course. Mom wasn't against her. I wasn't against her. Dodge wasn't against her. . . .

Hmmm. I thought about that while Dodge interrogated Mom's trash can with his snout. Dodge wasn't against Madame, but he *was* against her cats. There were a lot of them, some rumored to be as crazy as Madame herself.

"I'll look into it," Mom said, her sigh escaping. "Thank you for calling."

She set the phone down on the charger with an emphatic plunk. "Hi, guys," she said. "Never a dull moment. . . ." She pressed a button on her intercom. "Deb, could you arrange to have someone swing by Madame LeFarge's a little later? Maybe in a couple of hours? We don't want the woman thinking we're at her beck and call. . . ."

"Sure thing, Chief," Deb replied.

Mom disconnected and called to her assistant, Chase Langtree. Officer Langtree's broad shoulders arrived in her door frame in two seconds. "Hey, Cassie! Hi, Dodge!" he greeted, turning quickly to Mom. "You need something, Chief?"

Mom nodded. "Find out how Madame LeFarge got my direct line. I thought we took care of that. . . ."

Officer Langtree's green eyes were apologetic. "Sorry, Chief. I thought we did, too. I'll get on it."

I was petting Dodge and listening when Hero, Dodge's K-9 replacement on the force, walked into Mom's office. That might not sound like a miracle, but it was. When he first started at the station Hero was totally hyper, and until very recently — like right this second — he acted like a ridiculous puppy whenever Dodge was within sniffing distance (which, I might add, is a looong way for a dog). He'd whine, fidget, bow, wag, drool, you name it. He *never* just walked. . . .

At first Dodge and I didn't think there was any hope for the trainee. At all. But Hero and his police partner, Hank Riley, had provided essential backup on our last mission — the mission to end Mom's suspension from the force and bring in the crooks who killed Uncle Mark.

The night that all went down, Hero showed that he might have what it takes to be a great K-9 cop. Of course, he was still a rookie. It would take time for him to become the pro that Dodge was (and still is, unofficially). But Dodge and I both had to admit that Hero was earning his stripes.

"Hey, Hero," I said, still marveling that he wasn't knocking Dodge over. "How's it going?"

Hero gave me a pathetic look and dropped his head, wagging slowly.

Officer Langtree chuckled. "Not so good for our Hero. Riley's out of town, so he's been stuck in the office since yesterday afternoon. Riley'll be back later tonight, but . . ."

"Awww." My heart went out to the poor pup. No wonder he'd lost his wag. I bent down to gaze into his eyes. They weren't as dark as Dodge's, but they managed to convey every morsel of his misery. "Hey, boy, do you want to come home with us for a while?" I asked. Hero's tail lifted and he managed a slow wag; he definitely liked the idea. It wasn't going to go over big with Dodge, but I couldn't leave Hero cooped up at the station without his partner, could I?

I felt Dodge staring before I even turned around. The look he gave me was major, like I'd just told him we were out of kibble. Permanently. "Just for a little," I assured him, looking back to the rookie.

"Wanna?" I asked Hero again.

Hero let out a happy bark and scooted backward, his wag picking up speed. I gave Dodge an apologetic smile. We had company. "Well, all right, let's go!"

CHAPTER 2

I stared at Cassie, hoping she'd get the message. The "I don't want to hang out with Hero" message. Hero wasn't my pal. Or my partner. He was my replacement, for dog's sake!

But what did Cassie do? She ignored me! Not completely, but enough. Hero was coming with us. *Woof.*

I sat on my haunches and tried not to feel sorry for myself. Tried to think of good stuff. Like the yogurt lid I'd found in The Chief's trash. The one nobody saw me lick. I ran my tongue over my chops. Still tangy.

I wasn't happy to be leaving the station with Hero. Even if the whelp was learning. Even if he did help us out on our last case. He was still Hero. Still my replacement. Still an undignified pup.

"Let's go, team!" Cassie called cheerfully. Too cheerfully. We were not a team. But I went.

I couldn't blame Cassie. Or stay mad at her for long. Once my girl sank her teeth into an idea nobody could make her drop it — not even me. It was like barking up the wrong tree. A waste of time and woof power. And she couldn't help looking out for Hero, either. Cassie loved animals. Dogs in particular. That was why she worked at Pet Rescue after school. That was what made her a great human. Trouble was, she was *my* human. And I wasn't so big on sharing — especially with Hero.

I followed Cassie and Hero with my tail low. I caught up just as they headed out the door, and slid between them. I didn't want Hero to think he could claim my spot beside Cassie. It was bad enough that he was a temporary pack mate.

I shook off the bad feeling as best I could and raised my nose to the air. Cassie clipped on our leashes. (Hero's fault; I almost never wore a leash.) I remembered where we were going. I'd been listening at the station. I knew whose voice was buzzing in The Chief's ears. Madame LeFarge, the loon without feathers. The woman with thirteen cats. Thirteen yowling, smelly, useless cats! I pulled Cassie down the street toward the action.

9

"Dodge, no!" Cassie said, calling me back.

No? I stopped and turned. I saw Hero sitting calmly on the sidewalk. Since when did he do *that*?

My girl took a step closer and crouched. Looked me in the eye. "We've got to make our rounds," she said.

I had lots of rounds. Nightly rounds. "When Cassie was at school" rounds. Rounds with Cassie. But she wanted to make *our* rounds with Hero? Was she kidding?

"The seniors are waiting," she said.

Woof. Not kidding. And *woof.* The old-timers at Home Away from Home. Home Away was a den for older humans. Part of our weekly rounds. They loved it when Cassie and I visited. It perked them up. I loved it when we visited, too. Extra petting. And extra treats. *Mmmmm.* Treats. I loved treats. Treats were my favorite. I wagged.

Hero "wroofed." He probably loved treats, too. After all, he was a dog. But I didn't want to share my treats any more than I wanted to share my girl.

I stopped wagging. Cassie ruffled my fur and gazed right at me. "I know you weren't expecting to spend the afternoon with Hero. But he deserves a little break from the station, and I need you to rally. Okay?"

I licked her hand to show her I was in. I wasn't

happy, but I was in. And maybe, just maybe, I'd share my crumbs.

When we got to Home Away, the old-timers were in good spirits. One of my favorites, Duke MacLean, almost tackled me when we came through the door.

"Hey, Dodge!" He swooped in and grabbed me in a bear hug. Practically knocked me over. I stood my ground, though. Couldn't have the old geezer tackling me in front of the rookie. "How about a wrestle?" Duke asked.

Wrestle? Duke didn't wrestle. He tottered. I sat down to show him I wasn't playing. I dug Duke, I really did. He was completely bald. Smelled like coffee and grapefruit. Plus he knew how to pet a dog. Only he wasn't talking about petting. More like attacking. In a friendly way. Yeah. He wanted to play ruff. Which was fun except I didn't want to hurt the guy. He was old. And I had to set an example. For Hero. I looked over my shoulder and saw that Hero was following my lead. Sitting politely on his haunches. Miraculous.

"Okay, then." Duke took a swig of water. Then he dropped to the ground and started doing push-ups. "I haven't felt this good since the seventies!" he barked.

I let out a bark of my own and Esther looked up from her knitting. Esther was round and smelled like talcum powder and rose petals. She snorted a little whenever she laughed, which was a lot. She also had the best snacks in the place. *Mmmmm.* Snacks. I loved snacks.

I strolled over to Esther and licked her hand. It tasted like peanut butter. "Hello, Dodge," she said, stroking my bad ear. "Who's your friend?"

Cassie was still watching Duke. "You're fired up today. What's your secret?" she asked.

Duke hopped to his feet and winked at Cassie. Then he reached into his pocket and pulled out a bottle. "These little miracles," he said. He shook the bottle. It rattled like coffee beans in a can.

"They're called Pepper-Uppers!" Paul said as he ambled into the rec room. Paul was tall, skinny, and had the shakes. Maybe that was why he wore too much aftershave. He sat down in a chair beside Esther and smiled contentedly. "They're new senior supplements," he explained.

"Maximum omega-3 available!" Duke howled. "We've been giving them a trial run, and we like them so much we bought the company!" He sounded like the voices on TV commercials. Sold.

"Wow," Cassie said with a nod. "You're a great spokesman."

Paul raised a shaky hand. "That's the idea. The patent is pending, so we have exclusive access."

"They've changed my life," Duke declared as he popped off the lid and downed a few see-through ovals. He was acting like an excited puppy, and I was happy for the old guy. *Awoof!* No perking up needed today!

Next to me, Hero sniffed the carpet for dropped food. I sat down and turned my gaze on Esther. Waited patiently for her to bust out the good snacks. She kept oyster crackers and Peanut Butter Buddies in her purse. But sometimes she forgot how much I loved them. Or that they were there.

"Oh, Dodge. It's so good to see you," she whispered, still stroking my ear. Her fingers were soft and gentle.

"So you bought the Pepper-Uppers company?" Cassie was still questioning.

"Well, no. Not exactly," Paul replied. "But we did invest our retirement funds. I put in half my savings!"

"We're going to sell these beauties to other seniors," Duke explained. "We'll double our money in no time. Then we can get a pool put in here."

"And a hot tub," Paul added. He patted Esther's knee with a trembling hand.

I nosed Esther's purse to remind her about the goods at the bottom. She reached in and pulled out a package. *Woof!* Peanut Butter Buddies! I tried not to drool while she opened the plastic and dropped a couple on the ground. I started crunching them down. Peanut butter goodness! I was about to lick the crumbs when I heard Cassie gently clearing her throat. *Aw, woof.* I had to do the right thing. I stepped aside and let Hero lick the crumbs. But I didn't like it.

CHAPTER 3

"Thank you for coming," Esther said with a warm smile. "It's always so nice to see you." It was time to go, even if Duke wasn't finished trying to break his chin-up record in the Home Away courtyard.

"See you next week!" I called as the dogs started to pull on their leashes. Within seconds the two big shepherds were yanking me down the street. I knew I could get them on a heel — or Dodge, at least — but decided not to bother. Dodge was intent on getting to our next destination — a destination he'd had in mind since our stop at the station.

I could tell by his twitching ear that my dog had been listening in on Mom's telephone conversation. Dodge was always listening. That was part of what made him such a great detective. The two of us thought alike, and right now we were thinking about a visit to Madame LeFarge's. The old cat lady may have invented most of what she reported, but a stop at her house was never boring.

Of course, we'd have to keep an eye out for Bellport police officers. Mom had told me a billion times to stay away from Prospect Street, and especially Madame LeFarge. She was *not* someone the force wanted riled up. But could I help it if Dodge and Hero were dragging me there? They were pulling so hard I was sure I'd end up with gorilla arms.

"Woof!" Dodge barked, turning back to me for a quick second. He was asking to be let off his leash. The two of us rarely even *used* a leash, and right now it was cramping his style. He wanted to be free. Problem was, I didn't know Hero well enough to let them loose.

"Sorry, boy," I told him. "I've got to keep you two under control."

Dodge gave me a look, and I felt a twinge of guilt. He was often more in control than I was, and definitely better trained. "I know," I told him. "But thirteen cats are enough to make even the sanest dog crazy. Heck, maybe all of those cats are the reason Madame is so nuts!"

I snorted at my own joke. *Madame. Ha!* She was certifiably cuckoo. Even her name was wacky. I mean, *pardonnez-moi*, who goes by "Madame"? The old lady *might* have been French but was *surely* out of her head. Mom called her the town eccentric because as a Bellport official it was her job to be respectful. The rest of us just called her crazy.

As we turned onto Prospect Street the dogs strained even harder. "Easy, boys," I told them. I could see Madame's blue-shingled house with its turret and stained-glass windows up ahead. I could also see that something was going on — a cluster of people was gathered on the sidewalk. Madame was probably stirring up a pot of trouble, her specialty.

We hurried forward, keeping an eye out for police cruisers. As we drew closer I saw that the crowd of people was made up of neighbors, and they were gathered a couple of doors down from Madame's house. They were huddled next to a big truck with a fish painted on the side that was double-parked and half blocking the street. I scanned the crowd for Madame's tall frame and close-cropped gray hair, but she was nowhere to be found.

"It's been here for over an hour. Locked, with lights flashing," Henry Kales complained. Henry used to own the newsstand in town — a tiny shop with every news-paper, magazine, and candy you could think of — but had recently retired. His white hair was cut in a short buzz and his eyes were sad. He looked older than I remembered, but I hadn't seen him in a while. I stood within earshot while Dodge and Hero sniffed the nearby foliage. "The driver's disappeared," Henry reported. "I think we should call the police."

"You're starting to sound like Madame LeFarge," a woman in tight red curls snapped, waving her hand like she was shooing away insects. That had to be Erica Bloom, Madame LeFarge's next-door neighbor. "Next thing you know you'll be training your cats to poop in my yard, too," she complained.

Henry snorted and muttered something about cats under his breath.

I wanted to move in closer so I could hear more, but the dogs' noses were in overdrive — they didn't want to budge from their hedge. Making a quick decision, I dropped their leashes to the ground and stepped forward.

"So what if I sound like Madame?" Henry said, speaking up. "Someone has to be the voice of reason. For all we know there's a bomb in that truck."

The crowd shrank back slightly — everyone except Erica, who didn't seem concerned at all. Did she know something?

"You're all overreacting," she announced. "It's a waste of public money to involve the police in every little thing."

I nodded in agreement. The police had to deal with a lot of unnecessary stuff, and that took time and money. Mom talked about wasted resources all the time. But it wasn't that long ago that *Ms. Bloom* was the one calling the station, demanding that they get Madame's cats to stop trespassing and using her flower beds as a litter box. What were the police supposed to do, issue kitty restraining orders?

I raised my eyebrows and took another step closer. The feud between Erica Bloom and Madame LeFarge had been going on for a long time and wasn't likely to end soon. Everyone in town knew they'd never see eye to eye.

"I'd hardly call this a little thing," Henry objected. "Especially since Madame herself is missing."

Missing? That *was* odd, actually. I would have expected to find Madame right smack dab in the middle of the action, venting her theories and claiming conspiracy. An abandoned, double-parked truck would have drawn her like a magnet. I was pondering this and scanning again for her gray head when Hero started barking like crazy at a bright red shrub. Everyone turned at the sound of the bark. It was loud. It was ferocious.

It was the kind of bark a K-9 only used when he'd cornered a criminal.

CHAPTER 4

Hero was barking like a maniac, but I ignored him. I was busy tracing the paths of sneaky felines. Smelly trails ran from a gap in Madame's back fence through Erica Bloom's flower beds to the tall fence at the edge of Bloom's property. I remembered Bloom's complaints. Inappropriate use of neighbors' property. Poop in the petunias.

I sniffed out the evidence and noticed another smell. An oceany smell. Yeah. Something fishy. Then Hero's bark got *really* crazy. I had to find out what he was going on about.

I hoped it wasn't something silly. The pup was learning, but he still had a long way to go. I headed over in case he need backup. Cassie and the street crowd were gathered next to him by a tall bush. They smelled tense. Alarmed. Well, not Cassie. But everyone else.

"Leave it, Hero," Cassie called loudly. She picked up his leash and gave it a strong tug.

Hero's bark lessened but he couldn't stop. "Grrrowf." Something was in there.

Cassie crouched so she was on my level and we both stared intently into the branches. Yup. There was definitely something in there. Something that smelled like catnip.

"Call that mutt off!" a woman's voice screeched.

Mutt? What mutt? I stepped back a tiny bit and peered into the bush where the voice had come from.

Cassie put an arm on Hero's shoulder and he bit back his bark. It wasn't easy for him, though. His hackles were seriously raised. Catnip did that to a dog.

My nose was on overdrive, too, when Madame LeFarge emerged from the bush. "You've ruined it!" she howled. Her hair was covered in leaves and she was holding a camera.

I heard several people gulp. One gasped.

"What are you doing in Bill's bushes?" Erica Bloom demanded. She put her hands on her hips and stared down at Madame. Bloom was smaller than Madame, but she wasn't intimidated. She was mad. I half expected her to start circling. Or bite Madame on the neck. But Madame stared right back up at her. It was like watching an Akita and a miniature pinscher in a face-off. Neither one was likely to stop yapping.

"Are you all right? Let me help you." Henry Kales, the neighbor across the street, pushed through the crowd to assist Madame.

"Why are you worried about *her*?" Bloom balked. "It's bad enough having her thirteen cats sneaking around the neighborhood. Now she's trespassing, too!"

Kales ignored Bloom and held out a hand to Madame. She pushed it away and got to her feet herself. She growled at Bloom with her eyes.

But Bloom kept howling. "I finally get a good neighbor, and you're going to drive him away!"

Madame stamped her foot. She had on big, squishy shoes. The kind humans wore when they had to stand a lot. "My cats are angels, and good neighbor my eye!" she snarled. "That Bill Heinz is shifty and unreliable, and I'm going to prove it."

"Ladies, please!" Cassie stepped between them, and I pressed forward to back her up. It was risky to get between two snarling females. "There's no point in arguing."

"He's a scoundrel! Up to no good!" Madame went on, waving her hand at the house behind her.

"Your *cats* are up to no good!" Bloom shouted. "I don't see you trying to keep *them* under control."

Cassie was in over her head. These cranky women couldn't even agree to disagree! Madame tugged her shirt down and squared her shoulders. "I was waiting for the truck driver to return to his vehicle." Her words were short and sharp. Like a Chihuahua's bark. "His picture would have provided essential evidence to the police. But thanks to all of you, my stakeout has been shut down."

Bloom turned away in disgust. I swear I saw a light go off in the basement behind her. And I smelled something. That ocean smell. I put my nose down at the base of the bush and inhaled deeply. What was that?

"Grrr . . . ow!" *Bow wow OW!!* A sharp set of claws raked across my nose. Ripped into my flesh. I was a brave dog. I'd been hurt before. Plenty of times. But those claws were like razors!

I yelped and leaped back while one of Madame's cats streaked past. The menace who'd clawed me!

"Rowf!" I gave the little runt a warning bark. Then I was after her. "Rowf! Rowf! Rowf!" I was a trained K-9! Top of my class! I would not be mauled by a kitten!

Hero was on my tail, barking. "Wroof!" And I heard human shouts — Cassie's, Madame's, Bloom's. Cassie was calling me off. My training was calling me off, too. *Stop!* it said. My instincts disagreed. *Get her!* they told me. It wasn't really a fair fight because I was already running. Already chasing. And I was gaining on the little pest. . . .

Then, all of a sudden, the tiny tyrant ran right up a tree. *Aw, woof.* I hated that cats could do that.

The tabby climbed easily to a high branch and sat down. Just like that. She gazed at us. Twitched her tail. Hissed and smiled with her whiskers.

"Rowf!" I wanted to stop that tail from twitching. Bad.

"Wroof!" Hero did, too. But we could only bark at the injustice of built-in climbing equipment. Talk about an unfair advantage.

I heard Cassie behind me and stopped barking. But the growl in my throat wouldn't go away. "Grrrrrr."

I was staring up at the little beast when I felt a hand on my collar. Cassie. Her eyes were wide. She was worried. "Time to go!" she whispered frantically. "Madame is calling the police!"

I had no choice but to abandon my captive.

"Woof!" I barked at Hero to let him know. He whimpered, but turned away from the tree, too. Good dog.

Cassie was ahead of us, but not for long. The three of us hightailed it past Madame. "Yes, that's right," I heard her yap into the phone. "Feral dogs terrorizing the neighborhood."

Feral dogs? What was she talking about? There weren't any feral . . . then I remembered: This was Madame LeFarge. The loon without feathers.

Woof! I hoped it wasn't The Chief on the other end of the line.

CHAPTER 5

Even running at full tilt I couldn't keep up with Hero and Dodge — four legs were way faster than two. When I felt like my lungs would burst, I gave up and slowed to a walk, letting them race ahead, away from the mess on Prospect. They'd be okay. Dodge knew the way home and Hero would follow him anywhere.

My face was still sweaty and my heart still thudding when I looked up and saw her coming right toward me, walking her Maltese, Muffet.

Summer Hill.

Her name was like a bad joke because the girl was the exact opposite of actual summer. There was absolutely nothing warm or sunny or fun about her. Except maybe Muffet. Summer dressed her little pup in ridiculous outfits, but under the silly clothes Muffet was a rockin' pocket dog. Muffet also had a big crush on Dodge (proof of her excellent taste). I felt sorry for the Maltese, though. In addition to the fashion torture she inflicted, Summer was utterly dreadful.

I quickened my pace, hoping to turn onto Salisbury Drive before Summer spotted me and made some snotty remark (Summer was full of snotty remarks). But Summer must have sped up, too, because I ended up a lot closer to her than I thought I would. I could actually see her squinty blue eyes and wrinkled-up nose. Her lips were pursed and she looked like she was about to say something, so I did the only thing I could: braced for impact.

Then the weirdest thing happened. Summer opened her mouth and all that came out was, "Hey, Cassie." And then she sort of stared at me in a strange, distracted way.

Hey, Cassie? That was it?

I tried not to gawk. Summer hadn't said hello to me like a normal person in a gazillion years. "Oh, uh, hey, Summer," I replied as I turned onto my street. I could feel my forehead crinkling and I started to walk a little faster, half expecting a zinger to hit me between the shoulder blades. Only I heard . . . nothing.

Like I said, weird.

Up ahead, I could see the dogs romping on our lawn. I hurried up the sidewalk and dropped onto the grass. "Thanks for waiting, guys," I teased. Dodge licked my face in apology.

"Is that for chasing the cat or leaving me in the dust?" I asked.

"Whuff!" Dodge said, which I took to mean both.

"Apology accepted," I told him. "But that was close." We'd made it out of there before Madame could get the authorities to Prospect Street and bust me for breaking Bellport's leash laws. But I still felt guilty. How many times had Mom told me not to go near Madame's? A dozen? A hundred? A lot! I could totally hear her voice in my head. *The last thing that woman needs is an excuse to call the police!*

I reminded myself that we'd escaped getting caught and led the dogs into the house. It was my older brother Owen's turn to make dinner and my turn to set the table.

Dinner was required at 332 Salisbury Drive, and it was best to take care of your chores before The Chief had to remind you. Mom wasn't home yet, which was good. It meant I had a little time.

Inside, my little sister, Samantha, was on the couch poring over some teen magazine — the kind with quizzes to tell you how cool you are and pictures of celebs in matching outfits with verdicts about who wore it best. Her cat, Furball, purred on her lap. Samantha was ten but acted like a teenager: a little lazy and a lot self-absorbed. I hoped it was a phase but wasn't entirely convinced.

Doing my best to ignore her, I headed into the kitchen with the dogs. Miraculously, Hero didn't go straight for Furball. He stuck with us. Maturity points for that, no question.

Owen was just coming up from his basement room, bobbing his head to the music in his headphones.

"Whoa, visiting canine," he remarked a little too loudly, tilting his chin toward Hero. He peeked into the oven, where enchiladas were baking, and started to pull stuff for salad out of the fridge. I handed him the wooden bowl.

"Thanks," he said as the dogs lapped up water. I nodded and grabbed a stack of plates just as Mom pushed through the front door. She barely nodded as she took off her coat and headed straight to her office.

"Hi, guys. Let me know when dinner's ready," she called to us.

Not a good sign.

I set the table and started my homework while the dogs settled on the kitchen floor: crumb patrol. Lucky for them, Owen was a messy chef. Unlucky for them, all he dropped was lettuce. Then Dad got home and it was time for dinner.

The interrogation started the minute our napkins were on our laps. "Were you three on Prospect Street this afternoon?" Mom asked, looking at me.

I gulped. "Um . . . yes," I admitted.

Mom sighed and closed her eyes briefly before skewering me with a stern look. "I'm just getting things back under control at the station and you go and stir things up," she said pointedly. "Honestly, Cassandra. I expect you to know better."

I felt myself flush while Samantha snickered behind her hand. Dad was silent, eating his enchiladas. Owen, as usual, didn't seem to notice the rest of us were even there.

"Madame LeFarge is on a tear," Mom said. "She called the station four times today."

Owen smirked, giving himself away, and swirled his cheese around his knife.

"According to Madame, Erica Bloom is poisoning her cats, someone follows her whenever she goes out, and the new neighbor is up to no good. And after all *that* she reported dogs terrorizing the neighborhood." Mom waved her fork in the air, clearly exasperated. "That woman doesn't need any help from you and Dodge to ignite her overactive imagination!"

The dogs wiggled under the table and I stared down at my plate, feeling sheepish. Mom had only been back at work for a couple of weeks since her suspension. She had a lot of catching up to do, and a lot to deal with in general. And I had gone and tangled with Madame LeFarge. "I'm sorry," I muttered.

"Imagination isn't all bad," Dad offered.

Mom just glared. "I'm up to my eyeballs in work. The last thing I need is for my own kid to give Madame LeFarge a reason to call the station about feral dogs on the loose!"

"Oh, come on!" I objected. "Dodge and Hero are obviously not feral! Besides, what was she even doing hiding in the —" I didn't really mean to say all that, or raise my voice. I just sort of . . . did. I knew I was talking myself into a corner, but I couldn't seem to stop. "I mean, we were just out for a walk," I finished loudly, and lamely.

Mom got super quiet and I sucked in my breath. That had come out a lot sassier than I'd intended. I watched

Sam's eyes go wide and saw a hint of purple eye shadow on her lids. Like I said, ten going on sixteen.

"Why don't you walk the dogs and your dinner upstairs to your room," Mom said calmly. "Now."

My room? Harsh! But I knew I wasn't just being punished for talking back. I was being punished for my visit to Prospect Street. And for Mom's long day. For everything.

Dodge was already on his feet, his snout emerging from under the table. I pushed back my chair and silently carried my plate up the stairs. Hero passed me halfway up and I walked down the hall and into my room, my face burning with shame. I couldn't remember the last time one of us was sent away from the table.

I closed the door with my foot and put my quickly cooling dinner on the dresser. Dodge circled and lay down on his bed, his eyes watching me. I knew he felt bad, but I didn't blame him. I'd wanted to go to Madame's as much as he did.

"I guess we blew it," I said. A call to my best human friend was definitely in order. Hayley Gault was in my grade at Harbor Middle School and always good for an ear or a pep talk.

I was about to pull my phone out of my pocket when I noticed that things in my room weren't quite as I'd left them. Truthfully? I wasn't exactly a neat freak. But I definitely had a system and some super-honed powers of observation. I knew where my stuff lived, and could tell when it had been moved. Like now. The stack of mysteries on my desk was shifted to the right. The bottom drawer of my desk was open half an inch. The stuff on my shelf was leaning more than it usually did.

My eyebrows scrunched together. The only person in my house who would come into my room uninvited and mess with my belongings was my nosy little sister, Miss Sparkly Violet Eyelids, Samantha Sullivan.

I opened my mouth to scream her name, then clamped it shut. I'd been sent away from the table because of my lip, and yelling my head off would just make Mom angrier. I'd have to be patient and chew out Sam another time. Ugh!

Shoving a bite of cold enchilada in my big mouth, I plonked down on the floor. I gave Hero a pat and leaned into Dodge, glad to have company. At least we were all in the doghouse together.

CHAPTER 6

I lay down on my bed, and covered my nose with my paws. Not all the way — just a little. My snout still ached from the cat attack, but I didn't want to block the smell of dinner. I loved dinner. And hated fighting. Fighting made my ears lay flat.

The Mom had been really upset at the table. I hadn't seen her hackles raised like that since she got suspended. And to tell you the truth, I was a little embarrassed. After all, The Mom was The Chief. Top dog. Only she wasn't on her best behavior and we had a guest over. Worse. Her employee.

Hero cocked his head to let me know it was all right. We couldn't control human behavior. People were gonna do what people were gonna do. Plus they were both off the clock. He was right, but I still worried. I hoped the rookie hadn't lost any respect for The Chief. I hoped her Alpha position wasn't in question. And then there was my girl, Cassie. Her fur was pushed the wrong way, too.

"It's not like we meant to go looking for trouble," she grumbled as she took another bite of enchilada. It was cold — I could tell by the smell. Not as strong. "There were a bunch of people standing practically outside her house," Cassie said between chews.

Hero let out a guilty whimper, and I knew what he meant. We'd led her to Prospect Street like hounds on a hunt. So really it was *our* fault.

Cassie's phone rang, making my ears prick. Both of them. Sometimes my bad one acted like it was still good. Cassie set the half-eaten plate of enchiladas on the floor. *Mmmm.* Enchiladas. "Hello?" she said, and then, "Oh, hey, Hay. I was just going to call you."

I could hear the buzz of Hayley's voice through the phone. It was almost enough to distract me from the delicious dinner in front of me. Almost, but not quite. I loved enchiladas. Even cold ones.

"Yeah, right?" Cassie said into the phone. "It's great to have Mom back at work, but she's back on my case, too." She forked up another bite.

36

I struggled to pay attention to the conversation. To focus on Cassie telling Hayley what happened. But I already *knew* all about what happened. And . . . enchiladas!

Of course, I understood that the dinner on the floor wasn't mine. It was Cassie's. Except that food on the floor usually *was* mine. Or The Cat's. Or Mine. Floor patrol was one of my jobs. An important one. Clean floors were essential.

Cassie kept talking. "Yes. Seriously. In the bushes!" She reached over and gave me a pet, then used her foot to shove the plate in my direction. An invitation! For enchiladas! *Woof!* Did I mention that I *loved* enchiladas?

I got to my feet and took a nibble. *Mmmm.* Tortillas. Did I have to share with Hero? Another lick. Cheese. No, I didn't. Chicken. I'd already shared Esther's crumbs. Sauce. And Cassie had given her plate to *me*.

I was about to step to the side to block the plate when Hero got up and started sniffing. Not the plate of enchiladas. No. He was sniffing my bed. He'd found something. But, *mmmm.* So had my tongue. Chicken. Cheese. Tortillas. Enchiladas!

I could see Hero snuffling at the edge of my bed while I ate. I licked my chops. The only thing under there was . . .

Woof! Oh, no. Bunny! Bunny lived under there. Bunny, my sleep buddy!

Hero couldn't find Bunny. Hero couldn't *know* about Bunny. Ever! Cassie had given me Bunny and I'd unstuffed him myself. He was mine. I gulped down the last of the enchiladas. I turned and growled without licking the plate. Hero took a step back. I felt a little bad. I didn't usually talk to Hero like that. But Bunny was classified. Totally top secret. And I'd do whatever it took to keep him that way.

CHAPTER 7

I circled once, twice, three times. *Fwump!* I lay down on my bed and let out a breath. I loved my bed. It smelled like . . . me. I pulled out Bunny and gave him a sniff. I loved Bunny. Bunny smelled like me, too.

Hero was finally gone — retrieved by Riley. My tail thumped just thinking about it. Partly because I knew Bunny was safe. Partly because I knew The Mom's reputation was safe. And partly because I just wasn't a two-dog dog.

Cassie ran a brush through her hair and plopped into her bed. "I'm glad today is over," she mumbled. She burrowed under the covers. I was glad the day was over, too. Plus this was my favorite time of day. Snooze time. Quiet time. Cassie time.

I put my head on Bunny just as Cassie's hand dropped into my scruff. I exhaled slowly through my nose. *Woof.* I loved the feel of her fingers in my fur. I lay perfectly still, perfectly relaxed, waiting. Waiting for Cassie's breathing to change. Waiting for Cassie to fall asleep.

Sometimes I had to wait a long time. But not tonight. Her breathing slowed. It grew steady and deep. I stood slowly and nudged her arm up onto the bed. I licked her cheek. Time for nightly rounds.

I padded downstairs silently. I never knew who was going to be in the kitchen, even late at night. The Sullivan kitchen saw a lot of action. But tonight the coast was clear. I did a quick crumb check, then stood still, listening. The house was quiet.

I jumped up and caught the back door latch with my paw. *Click.* Got it on the first try. I hadn't always been so good at getting out — I had to learn. And catching the latch was only the first step. I kept the handle down while I hopped backward. That was the hard part. Then, when the door was open far enough, I slipped through. Got my tail clear. *Swish. Click.* I was out.

I trotted onto the lawn and inhaled the night air. Night air always smelled good. But it had been getting colder lately. Cold disguised smells — hid them under frosty layers. And it stung the inside of my nose. I raised it anyway and took a deep sniff. I picked up damp leaves. Dying grass. Wood smoke. Then I was ready. My paws moved fast over the lawn. A big leap and I was over the fence. I felt the chilly wind in my ears. *Awoof!* I loved nightly rounds. Most of Bellport was asleep. Most, but not all.

My snout throbbed slightly as I trotted down the side-walk. It still hurt from the scratch. Thinking about the scratch made me think about the cat who gave it to me. *Grrrr.* I hoped that cat got *stuck* in that tree. I hoped that cat was *still* stuck in that tree. I hoped so much I decided to check it out. I moved down the block, keeping my eyes peeled. My ears up. My senses on high alert.

I was on Prospect Street in a hurry. I padded over to the tree where the feline menace was last seen. But I knew she wasn't there. Knew because I didn't smell her.

Aw, woof. The little devil was probably lapping up a saucer of milk inside Madame's house. More injustice. I started across the street, my nose smarting. Then twitch-ing. I could smell Bloom's yard. Asters. Russian sage. Rotting leaves. I could smell cats, too. And that fishy ocean smell. Prospect Street wasn't near the ocean, though. And there wasn't even a lake or pond within sprinting distance. I sniffed again. It wasn't the fishy smell of cat food, either. I knew cat food and this was different. Deeply fishy. My nose quivered and a weird feeling snaked its way into my bones.

Something was strange. Wrong. Not right. I stopped in front of Madame's house. It wasn't a smell tipping me off this time, it was a sound. And a feeling. My hackles rose. The front porch light was dark, but the kitchen light was on in back. I slunk up the driveway for a closer look. Kept a low profile. I could really hear it now — the thing that was making me uneasy.

Yowling cats.

Cats were the worst. Besides the claws and the climbing, the lazy beasts never stopped meyowling for food. Only I knew that wasn't what these cats were meyowling about. Not this time.

Every hair on my back stood straight up as I stepped onto the back porch. The sound made me want to run but I forced myself to stay. *Stay.* I was a professional. I was trained. I would investigate.

I pushed my snout through the cat door. I tried to squeeze the rest of me in, too. But only my head and neck made it.

It was enough. Enough to see. And *really* hear. I whined at the sound, but the cats didn't notice. They were busy yowling and walking all over Madame. Yes. Walking on her. Their lady was on the floor. Not moving. Not responding to the howling and screeching. Not breathing.

This was bad. Really bad.

It looked like Madame was . . .

Rowf! I needed backup!

I yanked myself back through the cat door, grazing my scratched nose on the frame. I almost let out a yelp, but didn't. Not that the cats would have noticed. They were too freaked out to notice anything.

I must have been a little freaked, too. Because I bumped into a flowerpot. Hard. I lost my balance and half fell, tipping the pot off the stairs. *Crash!* It splintered on the cement walk below. So much for low profile.

I turned and raced down the driveway while the lights came on at Bloom's. "Who's there?" a voice called.

I didn't reply. I was already halfway down the block, racing home to get Cassie.

CHAPTER 8

"As if I'd ever socialize with a nobody like you." Summer sneered in my direction.

I stared at her, trying to think of a zingy retort. Nothing came to me. I wiped my face — it felt damp — and willed myself not to look away.

Something warm and wet slid across my cheek, and I smelled dog breath. That was weird. I put my hand out. Another slobbery swipe across my palm.

Dodge, I told myself in a sleepy haze. *It's Dodge. I'm dreaming.*

Or at least I *had* been dreaming. "Dodge, no." I pushed Dodge's snout away. I was fine with dog kisses most of the time, but . . . "It's the middle of the night!" I moaned.

I rolled toward the wall and pulled my knees up, willing both Summer and Dodge away. Summer faded, but Dodge took the covers in his teeth and pulled.

Dodge had never pulled my covers off before. Ever. So whatever he was trying to tell me had to be important. I rolled back over and sat up, rubbing my eyes.

"What?" I asked, shivering.

Dodge let out a sharp "Rowf!" Not his usual "woof." This bark meant business.

I put my hands on either side of his big square head and gazed into his brown eyes. "What is it, boy?"

His eyes widened slightly and he pulled away, backing toward the door. "Rowf!" Again, sharp and insistent.

"Okay, okay," I told him, getting to my feet. Whatever it was, it was serious. He wanted me to follow him. "I'm coming."

I pulled a pair of sweats over my pajama bottoms and shoved a mini-flashlight into my pocket. A rumbling sound made me stop for a second — the garage door. I hurried to the window in time to see Mom pulling out in the police cruiser. Only it wasn't just Mom; it was Mom *and* Dad. That meant something major was going on.

"Wow. Big-time, huh?" I looked at Dodge, impressed that he'd gotten the lead on this while I was sound asleep. "So what happened?"

Dodge shifted his weight from foot to foot and whimpered. Most of the time Dodge and I didn't need words — we could communicate with eye contact and body language. But every once in a while I wished we could just *talk*. Like right now.

"You'll just have to show me," I told him as we left our room. He led me down the stairs, first to my jacket, then to the garage. I hopped on my bike and followed him through the darkness, down Salisbury Drive and onto Elm. When we turned onto Prospect Street I immediately saw flashing lights — an ambulance in front of Madame's house. Mom's cruiser was parked next to the curb. I stopped pedaling and almost lost my balance.

"We can't get too close," I told Dodge as I hid my bike between a hedge and a garage several houses down. "We don't want to risk getting caught." We couldn't stay away, though, either. We snuck into Erica Bloom's yard and hid behind her potting shed.

It was a busy scene, I realized with a shudder. The first floor of Madame's house was lit up like a Christmas tree, and through the lace curtains I could see the shapes of the people working inside. Mom stood alone at her patrol car with her phone pressed to her ear, so I had to assume Dad was inside. Which meant . . .

I shook my head to clear it, pulled my hood up around my ears, and looked around at the people I *could* see. Erica shivered in her pajamas at the edge of her lawn, her face a mask. Across the street, Henry Kales stared at Madame's house like a zombie. A man I only half recognized approached Mom. He was short and skinny with a paunchy belly and bristly hair.

"That must be Bill Heinz," I told Dodge as I watched the new neighbor gesture with his hands. Dodge put his nose in the air and breathed in and out so deeply I could see his cheeks filling with air. "I'll bet you can read him from here," I said with a chuckle. "What's he smell like?"

Bill was nodding emphatically at Mom. He yawned and stretched. I wanted to decide that he seemed suspicious, but couldn't be sure.

Dodge and I sat there for a long time. Watching. Sniffing. Waiting. My butt got cold and my back got stiff. Bill stopped talking. Henry paced on the sidewalk. Erica went back into her house. "I wish we could get closer," I said with a sigh.

Dodge let out his own deep breath; we were in total agreement.

Finally Dad came out of the house with a stretcher and two EMTs. Dad was no stranger to stretchers; he was the town coroner. But tonight he looked grim. The body bag on top was all zipped up. It was what I'd suspected but didn't want to believe.

Dodge's nose twitched and he let out a whimper. I scooted toward him and wrapped an arm around his neck. Only one person had lived in that house — the one coming out in a bag.

"Oh, Dodge." I gulped. "Madame LeFarge is dead."

CHAPTER 9

I smelled the plastic body bag before Cassie saw it. And I knew. I guess I knew from the moment I stuck my head through the cat door. I'd encountered dead bodies before. Only this time I didn't want to know.

But now Cassie'd said it out loud. Madame was dead. Now I knew it and felt it. Cassie put her arm around me. We felt it together.

Then I felt something else. My nose. It tingled. Something brushed my tail. I twitched it off, not really paying attention. I smelled dust and thyme. A familiar yowl made my spine stiffen. It was my attacker's yowl. The reason I'd come to investigate in the first place! But that was before a body was put in a bag.

I stared as the body was loaded into the ambulance. The Dad climbed in behind it. He was the coroner. Bodies in bags were his job. We watched them drive away, Cassie and I.

The taillights disappeared and I turned to watch The Chief. She was talking to Kales. He looked like he'd been kicked. Like he needed to find a quiet spot to lick his wounds.

"So you were the one who found her?" The Chief asked. She wrote stuff on a pad of paper. Kind of like Cassie's notebook, only smaller. Kales nodded. Answering and not answering. There but not there.

"I heard a crash and went over," he said. "She usually yells at me to get away from her porch the minute I step off the sidewalk. But this time there was no yelling. Just the cats . . ."

I wondered if the crash was the flowerpot I'd knocked over. Kales wasn't the first one to find Madame. I was. Right after her cats. And maybe someone else.

The Chief asked more questions but didn't get much out of the neighbors. She'd be done soon. Nothing else to dig up tonight. A little bit of light was starting to show in the sky. I nudged Cassie under the chin with my muzzle.

Her arm was still around my neck, the way I liked it. But we needed to move.

"Right. We should go," she whispered. She got to her feet and walked stiffly to her bike. She kept to the darkest shadows. I kept close to her side.

By the time we got home, the sun was getting ready to rise. We were dog tired. Cassie took a shower while I waited outside the door. Tile floors weren't for dogs, unless it was hot.

The Mom and The Dad were both home when we went downstairs. They looked like old tug toys. Chewed up and stretched out.

"We got an emergency call late last night," The Mom reported to the pack as they ate their cereal. It wasn't a pancake morning. There would be no bacon.

"Madame LeFarge is dead." The Chief wrapped her paws around her coffee mug. Steam rose in front of her face.

"What? How?" Cassie gasped. She sounded surprised. She sounded like we hadn't just watched the whole thing. She was a top-notch actress. Good Cassie.

The Dad nodded and let out a big breath. He didn't seem as sad as The Mom. He liked a body. Spent a lot of time with them. "I've ordered an autopsy," he said. "The emergency call warrants it. But it looks like she just slipped and fell in her kitchen."

The Mom's forehead got all bunched. Cassie looked surprised all over again, for real this time. There was no tangy lie smell in the air like there was a minute ago. She looked a little disappointed, too. I was with her. We were both thinking: *Slipped and fell in her kitchen?* That was not how a lady as crazy as Madame would die.

No. Way.

CHAPTER 10

On Saturdays Dodge and I always went to Pet Rescue, the shelter where I volunteered. Pet Rescue was one of my favorite places on the planet, and helping find forever-families for animals was one of the best things I did, right behind detective work with Dodge. But after our all-nighter on Prospect Street, I was beat. My eyes were scratchy and I had a throat tickle. I was seriously tempted to skip Pet Rescue and kick it on the couch. But I knew those fuzzy orphaned faces at PR were counting on me, and I had a feeling that sticking to my regular routine might help me shed the uneasy feelings I'd been having about Madame.

I wasn't sure if he was picking it up from me or feeling it himself, but Dodge seemed tired and creeped out, too. He usually loved going to PR, and raced ahead and wagged at the front door. But today he hung back all droopy tailed. Not wagging. Not whining. Just looking. It was like the shelter was emitting Dodge repellent or something.

"Come on," I coaxed. He came, but reluctantly. And the minute I opened the door I understood why. In fact, I probably should've heeded Dodge's warning.

"Cassie! I'm so glad you're here!" Gwen called desperately from behind the reception desk. Gwen practically ran Pet Rescue and was usually unflappable. She could mop up a puppy puddle with one hand, fill out adoption forms with the other, and never let her latte get cold or her community college homework go undone. She was on top of things.

But not today.

Today Gwen's pink-streaked hair was hanging in her face, and even through the fringe I could tell she was frazzled. There were three takeout coffee cups on the counter, all half filled with cold caffeine. "We just got thirteen new animals — all cats!" she explained, shaking her head. "And they are *not* happy about it."

"Thirteen cats," I murmured as I wheeled my bike into a corner. The felines could only be Madame's. That must have been what Dodge was trying to tell me. Madame's cats had all been delivered to Pet Rescue!

"Sorry, boy," I told Dodge. "I got you now. You can stay here." The lobby was probably the best place for him to hang today — away from the new charges. Dodge was tolerant enough of Furball, Sam's cat. But Madame's cats were pretty . . . catty, and the insult on Dodge's nose was pretty fresh.

I followed Gwen to the back room, where the cats were going bonkers, yowling and twitching their tails.

Madame had names for each of her kitties, but we had no idea what they were and there was no one to ask. Gwen, in her no-nonsense way, redubbed most of them with temporary spice names. She walked me past Ginger, Mustard, Curry, Parsley, Sage, Cinnamon, and Cayenne. I gave a few small pets to the poor orphans through the metal mesh, but opening the cages was totally off-limits. The cats were so freaked out and cranky they would have bolted for sure. Some of them looked kind of scraggly, too. Stress, I guessed.

Gwen pushed her hair out of her face and right away I saw the worry in her gray eyes — it was going to take a miracle to find homes for so many ornery, scrappy-looking adult cats.

"Don't worry. We'll get them all adopted," I assured her.

"It's not just that," she said. "It's these guys." She pointed to two cages near the end of the row. "I'm calling them Salt and Pepper. They're sick, and I've never seen anything like it before. Dr. Byrnes doesn't know what's wrong, and isn't sure they'll make it. They could be contagious."

I bent down to check out Salt and Pepper. Their coats were dry and matted and they were lying awkwardly, not even curled up. They seemed like they barely had the energy to breathe. "Oh, no!" My heart went out to them.

At PR we saw lots of animals that weren't well. Fleas, ticks, mange, bites, scratches, broken limbs, sometimes worse. That's why we had Dr. Byrnes, a full-time veterinarian, on staff. She could stitch up a wound in no time and diagnose just about anything. But Salt and Pepper looked bad. Neglected — not at all like they'd belonged to an über cat lover like Madame.

"I know." Gwen nodded when she saw my face. "And then there's this one." She pointed to an upper cage where a small white paw with claws extended was poking through the door. "This little thing is a disaster! She's young and super high-strung. She really needs to be fostered — get a little socialized — but she's all teeth and claws!"

On the other side of the wire mesh sat a youngish orange-striped tabby with white socks. Totally adorable. She pulled her paw in and I reached toward the cage, talking in a soothing voice to see if I could calm her down. She arched her back and sidestepped away from the door, hissing. Not the kind of behavior that got a cat adopted. . . .

"See? I haven't even been able to check her vitals," Gwen said.

"How about the towel trick?" I offered to wrap the little terror up and hold her for the quick exam. It was a technique we used with biters and scratchers, and it worked pretty well. Usually.

With my hands and wrists wrapped I opened the cage, blocking the exit. The tabby was a whirlwind of claws, but I managed to grasp and wrap her up in my terry-cloth armor.

She was a fighter. I could feel her body writhing inside the towel and struggled to keep her from wiggling free. I kept a tight hold on her while we walked to an examination room, and she still managed to push her little orange face through the folds.

"It's all right," I tried to tell her as I stepped into the lobby and — oh, man, I totally forgot that was where

Dodge was waiting! Dodge stood up quickly, so I held the little cat even tighter and raised my arms.

And then the weirdest thing happened. When the cat saw Dodge she did just the opposite of what I expected. Instead of freaking and trying to escape, she calmed right down! I thought maybe she was frozen in fear or that I'd squeezed too hard. But when I lowered her a little to see if she was okay, she stretched her head out of the towel and touched her tiny pink nose to the end of Dodge's big black snout.

CHAPTER 11

The second the feline nose hit mine I knew I was face-to-face with the tiny slasher — the kitten who'd sliced my nose. Her dust and thyme smell gave her away. I pulled back in a hurry. I didn't want to get my tender snout ripped again.

Grrrr. I remembered the sharp insult of her claws. My lips curled back. I could eat that kitten for a snack! But the menace arched out of the towel Cassie had her in. She reached her neck farther and licked my nose with her rough tongue. No kidding — she licked me!

The sandpaper kiss hurt. A little. But that wasn't what put me in a stay. I was stunned. I could not move. It was the first time I'd seen a cat apologize. Ever.

While the shock wore off, the kitten did the happy little growl cats do. I shook a bit, to make sure this was happening. Yeah. It was happening. She'd attacked me. And now she was glad to see me. The cat was as crazy as her woman — her dead woman.

Woof. That thought set me back on my haunches. I knew how it was to lose your human. *Ruff.* The bite went right out of me. All I could do was sit.

Cassie and Gwen looked shocked, too. All they could do was stand. With their mouths open. Then Cassie set the cat down on the floor. The stripy kid walked up to me, bold as a boxer. Like we were pack mates. She rubbed against me. She wove in and out of my front legs.

"She likes you," Cassie gasped. A smile was spreading across her face. The first Cassie smile I'd seen since our late-night investigation.

"Likes? Loves!" Gwen cried. She closed one of her eyes, then opened it. Quickly. I'd seen humans do that before. It meant they had a little joke. A little secret. Only I didn't know what it was. I didn't get it.

"I guess we found our foster family!" Gwen said. She elbowed Cassie. Cassie's smile got even bigger.

Now I got it. *Oh, woof.* I got it all right.

When Cassie's shift was over, we didn't leave PR alone. Guess who left with us?

"I'm so glad you're taking her," Gwen said. She handed Cassie a bag of kitten food. The tiny pest was on my heels. She hadn't been more than a tail's length away from me since Cassie set her down.

"That little cat is bananas," Cassie said with a laugh. "In fact, I think that's what I'm going to call her: Bananas!" Then she looked at her bike. And the bag of kitty kibble. "But, uh, how am I going to get her home?"

My drooping tail perked up. I was saved! Cats don't do long walks. The little twerp would have to stay behind! Then *bow-OW!* Again with the claws. The stripy kid was on me. Actually *on* me. Like I was a horse.

Cassie and Gwen cracked up. I couldn't even look at them.

"Aw, Bananas is hitching a ride!" Cassie cried. Her voice told me that she thought it was great, even if I didn't. Like it or not, I was helping out. And I couldn't let my girl down. I stood up straighter so the hitchhiker wouldn't slip. The Kid held steady, and it didn't hurt . . . too much. Still, totally degrading. But Cassie was smiling. *Woof.*

CHAPTER 12

I stood at the base of the tree, ready to climb, happy to be back. But as my foot hit the bottom rung of the ladder I heard something so wrong it stopped me in my tracks. There were voices, more than one, coming from our secret fort.

"Who's up there?" I called, suspecting that Sam had snuck her friends into our clubhouse. But it wasn't Sam. It was worse *than* Sam.

"Oh! Cassie!" Summer's head peeked over the edge of the platform. She looked flushed. Embarrassed, even. Which didn't make any sense. It was Summer's fort. Our fort. Our secret *fort.*

What was going on?

"Summer?" I felt my brow wrinkle with confusion.

"Hi, Cassandra. I, uh, didn't know you were back from your grandparents' already."

"Really?" I said, still confused. I heard my voice in my head but couldn't make it come out of my mouth. How could you not know? We had a whole plan for my first day back. I brought you shells from the beach, and the mystery I finished in the car that you'll totally love, and . . . *I could only stand there, frozen, at the bottom of the ladder.*

"Guess what?" Summer asked, still gazing down at me like some kind of specimen in the zoo. Her blue eyes sparkled icily. Were they always that cold? "I initiated Eva and Celeste into our club. And we thought of a new name!"

"A better one!" another voice said. One of the intruders.

Two more heads appeared over the edge of the wooden floor, Eva's pixie cut and Celeste's long pigtails — both blonde, just like Summer. The three of them squinted at me — a tiny brown rodent far below. Summer held something in her hand.

"Oh, and they just love our book," Summer chirped.

"Yeah. Your detective notes are hilarious!" Celeste said, snickering. Then they laughed, all of them, so hard they had to back away from the edge so they wouldn't fall.

Hilarious? My notes?

They weren't supposed to be.

*　　*　　*

I could still hear the sharp peals of laughter echoing in my head when I opened my eyes. I closed them again, tightly, to try to squeeze out the dream. When I reopened them, Dodge was gazing at me with a worried puppy face.

"Was I talking in my sleep?" I asked. He gave me such a sorrowful look that I patted the mattress beside me. Mom wasn't crazy about dog hair on the sheets (or the couch), but sometimes you just need to cuddle your dog.

Dodge crawled up, being careful not to wake Bananas, and gave me a lick on the cheek.

"Thanks," I whispered as he hunkered down beside me.

I peered over Dodge's shoulder at the orange cat curled up with Bunny on Dodge's bed. It was such a crazy sight I wondered if I was still dreaming. A cat. With Bunny. On Dodge's bed. What the heck?

We'd only been fostering Bananas for two days, but the wacky kitten had made herself right at home. And the strangest part was that Dodge was totally putting up with it. Enjoying it, even.

Dodge was fairly feline tolerant for a canine. He put up with Furball, who could be a lot to take. Still, he was definitely *not* what you'd call a cat lover. I'd actually been worried about leaving him home with two cats while I was at school. But now that I'd seen Bananas sleep on Dodge's head and curl up next to him? I knew my worries were unnecessary. I smiled at the miracle of it — Dodge was full of surprises — and buried my face in his scruff.

We were still snuggling when Bananas woke up and realized she was alone on Dodge's big bed. She gave a cat stretch and leapt up beside us, snuggling as close to Dodge as possible before nestling down and going back to sleep. Amazing.

The bad dream was fading into a distant memory when Sam passed my partially open door. I barely caught a glimpse of her sparkly sneakers but she was back in a flash, framed in my doorway and staring in disbelief at the cat and dog pile on my bed.

"Aw. Who says cats and dogs can't be friends?" she crooned.

"I know, right?" The cuteness was proof that animals could overcome differences. Still, if Sam thought that Dodge and *Furball* would ever get this cozy, she'd need to think again. Those two would never be anything but enemies.

"You'd better get going," Sam told me. "It's almost eight."

I squinted at her — I hated it when she told me what to do — and waited for her to disappear again before tossing the covers aside and getting out of bed. Bananas rolled over and stretched a paw over Dodge's leg.

"You two snuggle bunnies can just stay here," I told Dodge quietly. "I'll leave your kibble in your bowl and see you when I get home from school."

He whimpered quietly but didn't move thanks to Bananas and her kitty grip.

Fifteen minutes later I was out the door with a cereal bar and an apple. I took a bite of fruit and glanced at my phone to see if Hayley had texted. No messages, just one missed call. I looked at the caller ID, then looked again. It was from Summer!

I hit delete and shuddered. I'd just been dreaming — or nightmaring — about her, and then her name was on my screen. The relatively friendly hello the other day was strange enough. Now she was calling, too? Was she stalking me? Setting me up for something embarrassing? I shoved the phone in my pocket and took another bite of apple, telling myself that she'd misdialed. Or that Muffet was trying to call Dodge. (Okay, I knew that was impossible, but it somehow made more sense.) Summer's name popping up on my phone was just plain weird.

I picked up my pace, not really wanting to investigate that particular mystery, and hurried to catch up with

Alicia and Hayley in the schoolyard. With just five minutes before the bell, I wasted no time filling my two best friends in on the Madame LeFarge situation.

"Wait, she's called *Madame*? Are you serious?" Alicia stared at me like I was the crazy one. Being relatively new to Bellport, she didn't know who Madame LeFarge was.

"Oh, she's the town cat lady," Hayley explained.

"What's a cat lady?" Alicia asked. Apparently they didn't have those in Somalia and Cambodia, where Alicia's family lived before, when her parents worked in the Peace Corps.

Hayley explained that cat ladies were nice-but-nutty women who collected stray cats. "They usually end up living with a *lot* of animals."

"Madame only had thirteen," I said.

"*Only* thirteen?"

"And she wasn't that nice. She was mostly, um, difficult." I told Alicia about Madame's paranoia and crankiness, and how she was hard to deal with. "She had lots of crazy conspiracy theories and called the station all the time to report ridiculous stuff. The last time I saw her she was doing her own stakeout on an illegal double-parker. A one-woman shakedown!"

Hayley smiled and shook her head. "She was always onto something."

Alicia tapped a finger on her chin. "So this Madame LeFarge collected cats, conducted stakeouts, and made crazy reports?"

I nodded. "Yup."

"And then one night she just fell in her kitchen and died?"

Hearing Alicia say that out loud totally shed a spotlight on why Madame's death wasn't sitting right. She wasn't some feeble old lady. She was cantankerous, strong, spry, and annoying — the kind of person who hid in the bushes and leapt out at you in a rage — not exactly an "I've fallen and I can't get up" candidate. There had to be more to this story, and I suddenly wanted to pull out my notebook, sit down with Dodge, and get to the bottom of it. I wanted to take the case. Unfortunately, the bell was ringing and I had to take my seat in homeroom instead. Detective work would have to wait until lunch.

When Hayley and Alicia came into the lunchroom three hours later, I was sitting alone, hunched over my notebook, furiously scribbling notes. I was so absorbed in logging details and suspicions about Madame's neighbors that I barely looked up.

"Um, hello?" Hayley said, sliding her tray onto the table next to mine.

"Hey," I replied distractedly.

She peered at my open notebook. "Annoyed enough to kill?" she read.

"Sounds juicy," Alicia added as she took her seat across from us. She opened a container of garlic-and-ginger-scented noodles and twirled up a bite. Her lunches made even the cafeteria smell appetizing.

"Local woman killed by mob of fed up neighbors," Hayley said dramatically, reading an invisible headline.

I chuckled and put my notebook away. Lunch was too short to eat, talk, *and* take notes. I opened my yogurt and had barely swallowed my first bite when Hayley sent an elbow into my ribs and almost made me choke.

"Trouble at eleven o'clock," she whispered, pointing with her chin.

I looked across the room and spotted Summer picking at her lunch. Eva and Celeste, her look-alike BFFs, were in a platinum huddle, ignoring their leader. Summer sat there with her ice-blue eyes laser-locked on *me*. I felt a chill, remembering the hello and the missed call. I knew in my bones that something was going on — something I'd have to investigate. The wheels in my head started spinning so fast that I accidentally did something really stupid. I returned Summer's gaze. And then what did *she* do? She kind of, sort of, smiled at me.

What the heck?

Smiling at me was *not* normal Summer behavior. Summer sneered. Summer scowled. She raised her snotty nose and turned the other way, muttering nasty things behind my back.

A friendly Summer was more terrifying than global warming.

My mouth must have dropped open in shock, because Hayley reached out a finger and lifted my chin, closing it. "Keep it together, girlfriend."

"What gives?" Alicia asked, clearly confused. "Doesn't she hate you?"

"Yes," I answered. "Definitely. A lot." If Sherlock had Moriarty, I had Summer Hill. My archenemy. My nemesis. The bane of my existence.

But a little voice in my head added: *She didn't used to be.*

CHAPTER 13

Ka-woof! I sneezed. *Ka-woof! Ka-woof!* Again and again. Probably cat fuzz. I hated cat fuzz. I hated sneezing, too. Only I didn't mind this sneezing fit too much. Because the fuzz making me sneeze was Banana fuzz. Not the fruit, the kitten. The Kid had gotten under my skin.

I told myself I wasn't crazy. That she was more dog than cat. I'd even collected evidence to prove it. For example, she liked to fetch the little ball The Brother threw for her. She liked eating kibble (hers *and* mine). And she hated The (Other) Cat, who hated her back. See? Hard evidence!

Of course The Cat had no idea how to be welcoming. Not even to a guest of her own kind. I wasn't crazy about welcoming a kitten into our pack. At first. But The Cat acted like it was the end of the world. She arched and walked sideways every time she saw Bananas. She hissed and spat even though she was twice The Kid's size. Talk about crazy!

After Cassie left for school we hung out — me and Bananas — at the house. Part of me was itching to get out for rounds. But I couldn't leave The Kid with The Cat. She needed me. And, well, she was good company.

I followed Bananas around while she explored. She found a patch of sun big enough for both of us and we flopped. Sun was nice. Sun could be a new favorite. I soaked up the rays while she licked my sore nose. Then it was time for lunch.

Whenever I saw The Cat leap on the counters or walk on the back of the couch I felt jealous. I thought it was wrong. But The Kid showed me it could be right. She leaped on the dryer and knocked the box of treats to the ground. We shared. Then we destroyed the evidence.

When Cassie got home from school, playtime was over. Cats liked to lounge — even Bananas. Lazing and lounging had been fun. But I liked to work. Plus I could tell Cassie had a job for us.

"Go time, Dodge," she told me. "We're taking the Madame LeFarge case."

I let out a bark. "Woof!" I loved a case. I couldn't wait to get started.

The Kid yowled when she saw that we were headed out without her.

"We're going to your house to find out what happened to your lady," Cassie explained.

We were? I knew we needed to go back there. But nothing good had come out of our recent visits to Prospect Street. So I sat down fast. Maybe I whined.

"Don't worry, Dodge," Cassie said. "Madame can't call the police on us anymore." Then she sighed.

Right. Madame wasn't there. That was why *we* needed to be. That was why we were on the case.

By the time we hit Prospect my lounginess and hesitation were gone. My eyes and ears were on high alert. We didn't want to be noticed, so we moved slow and steady. Just a dog and his girl out for a stroll. On the outside, anyway. On the inside we were collecting data.

I started with a nose scan at the crime scene. Madame's house smelled like it did before, only staler. Cat food. Cat fuzz. Cat box. The cats were gone but their stink remained. And their mess.

Cassie tried the back door. Locked. The broken flowerpot was right where I'd knocked it. I stuck my head through the cat door while Cassie checked for open windows and poked around outside. I tried again to get a shoulder through the small passage. No go. I'd have to investigate as best I could with just my eyes, nose, and ears.

My nose quivering, I looked around. I saw cat climbing towers. Hair-covered cat beds. Bowls and bowls of old cat kibble. Stale and dry — only a little tempting. I smelled all the cat smells. *Woof.* And something else, something . . . fishy.

I pushed harder against the tiny opening, willing myself to be dachshund size, hoping I wouldn't get stuck. That's when I saw something new. Out of the corner of my eye. I streeeetched my neck as far as I could. I opened my mouth and managed to get a tooth on it. The thing rolled closer and I picked it up gently. It was a bottle. Plastic. It reeked of cat spit and fish. Tasted like it, too. *Slurp.*

I pulled back, leaving a little hair behind. I dropped the bottle on the doorstep before giving it a final lick. It was small and covered in teeth and claw marks. Empty. The opening was chewed. I pressed my snout into it and smelled that deep fishy smell. Then I picked it up and gave it to Cassie.

My girl turned it over. She wasn't sure it was a clue. Neither was I. She wiped her paws on her jeans. Her eyebrows came down. Puzzled. Then they went up. Alarmed. We'd been spotted!

"You there!" somebody yelled at us.

My hair stood on end and I froze in my tracks.

"Hide!" Cassie hissed.

We ran off the steps toward a small shed with the garbage cans. They were ripe, filled with kitty litter. *Oh, woof.*

CHAPTER 14

"What are you doing in my neighbor's yard?" a voice snapped. Erica Bloom's. We'd been spotted!

I whirled around, panicked. Erica was peering through the boards of her fence, her red curls bobbing just above it. I couldn't see her face or the rest of her body, but was sure she was wagging a finger at us. We were caught, stuck in Madame's backyard — the only escape was around the side of the house, and it would definitely include a lecture about trespassing. Unless . . .

I grabbed a garbage can from the shed in the side yard and started to pull it to the curb. "Woof!" Dodge barked. I put my hand on his head to quiet him down.

"We came to pay our respects," I called out, pausing to rub my eyes and put on my best sad face. "I wanted to see if there was anything I could do to help — like getting the trash out. I — I just can't believe she's gone." I rambled, stuttering and sniffing to smooth Erica's ruffled feathers. Hardly anyone would scream at a sad kid.

I dragged the trash can down the path along the fence, hoping my plan would work. It did. By the time I got the smelly garbage to the sidewalk at the front of the house, Erica's hackles were down, and so were Dodge's.

Erica stood listlessly next to her own can of refuse. "It's funny. I never thought I'd be sad to see her go," she said.

I practically choked. That was the *last* thing I expected to hear from Erica Bloom. Based on everything I'd heard, she *hated* Madame. I felt my eyes narrow, and all I could think about was how much Erica complained about her neighbor. How angry she was the night Madame hid in the bushes . . . the night Madame *died*.

I glanced down at Dodge, who was sniffing up a storm. Was he getting this?

Erica was the top entry on our *Annoyed Enough to Kill?* list. Her ongoing feud with Madame was legendary. This "sad to see her go" stuff had to be an act, and I wanted to get her to break character. "I know what you mean," I offered, playing along.

"It's bizarre, but I actually miss her. I even miss her cats — well, a few of them."

"It's just terrible," I said consolingly.

"Terribly surprising," she admitted, tugging a curl. "Have you ever known someone who drives you crazy, yet who you still sort of care about?"

That made me stop, because I had to admit I did. "Yeah, like a frenemy. Or my sister," I offered. But even though I knew what she meant, I was still suspicious. I wanted to go back to Madame's backyard, or check out her shed, or see what Dodge was sniffing up. But Erica just stood there, awkwardly, waiting for us to leave. "Well, we'd better get going. See you," I finally said. I called to Dodge, who was busily searching for evidence.

I thought Dodge would come right to me like he usually does, but when Erica turned and started up her walk he jumped up and put his paws on the rim of her trash can. He called my attention to the corner of a plastic bag bulging out. I took a few steps back and tried to get a closer look without letting Erica see that I was snooping.

The bag was from a hardware store or plant nursery. STEDI-GRO WITH FISH EMULSION, it said on the front. It was mostly full, and I wondered why Erica was throwing it out. Wasn't fancy fertilizer kind of expensive? Then the small print caught my eye. Down in the corner there was a label with the word CAUTION in capital letters. Below that it read KEEP OUT OF REACH OF CHILDREN AND PETS.

My heart started to race. I kept one eye on Erica's retreating form, blocked the trash can with my body, and reached for the bag. But just then Erica turned. Rats! She had that look teachers got when they caught you passing notes in class — stern and disappointed. "I thought you were going," she snapped. Her friendly mood had disappeared.

"I am!" I replied with a smile. "Just getting my dog!" Unfortunately, Dodge was now ahead of me, trotting down the sidewalk toward home. *Oops!*

"Woof!" Dodge barked for me to hurry.

Erica turned his way, squinting. Probably remembering that he was one of the "feral" dogs from the other night. But while her attention was turned, I seized my chance. I grabbed the warning label, tore it off, and shoved it into my pocket.

Erica looked like she was about to say something, but I didn't give her the chance. I hurried to catch up with Dodge, feeling the curly-haired woman's eyes on my back as the caution label flashed in my head.

Dodge lifted his nose and sniffed the air as we walked away. I did, too. I was pretty sure I smelled something — something fouler than fish emulsion. Maybe Madame hadn't had such a great imagination. Maybe she hadn't imagined anything at all.

More investigating was definitely in order, and I knew where we had to dig next. "Come on, Dodge. Let's go see Dad."

CHAPTER 15

I didn't see him until we were leaving. Kales, across the street on his front porch. Staring at Madame LeFarge's house. Sitting. Staying. Staring.

"Whuff," I barked softly to let Cassie know. Only Cassie. Not Bloom, who was huffing about us getting too close to her fishy garbage.

Cassie heard me. "What is it, boy?"

I lifted my snout toward Kales. And she saw.

"Henry Kales," she murmured. As soon as he saw us Kales got up. He went inside and the door banged shut behind him.

"Interesting . . ." Cassie murmured. That guy was always watching. What did he see?

We would just have to wonder. Cassie wasn't sticking around to find out. She was following her instincts, and I was following her. Downtown. I thought we might be headed to the station. The Mom's office. But Cassie turned before we got there. We weren't headed for The Mom's office. We were headed for The Dad's. *Woof!*

The Dad's office was full of smells. Dead was as smelly as it got, and his office was all about dead. The Dad was the town coroner. He was a kind of detective, too.

The Dad investigated a body to find out how long it had been dead. Where it got dead. Why it got dead. How it got dead. All kinds of stuff. He was good at his job.

We walked into the front office. It had a desk. Files. Computers. No water bowl, though. Not like the station. A woman typed at a computer. She smelled like doughnuts and mothballs. She started to tell Cassie that dogs were not allowed. Then she realized who she was talking to. Cassie wasn't just any girl, and I wasn't just any dog.

"Cassie! Haven't seen you here in a while. I'll get your dad," she said. She walked back to the place where the dead smells came from. Cassie shifted her weight from foot to foot. She smelled nervous. Like grapefruit. Then The Dad came out to see us.

"If it isn't the best crime-fighting team on six legs!" The Dad hugged Cassie. He ruffled my fur. Then he led us back to the room where people ate lunch — a small room with a refrigerator in it. And a microwave that needed a thorough licking. The floor had old crumbs — as old as me. They needed a good dog around the place. While Cassie and The Dad talked, I did what I could.

"So what brings you to the Dead Zone?" The Dad joked.

Cassie stood stiffly, still smelling tangy. Her invisible tail was tucked between her legs. "We were in the neighborhood," she mumbled. It was true. We *were* in the neighborhood. But we'd walked a long time to get here.

The Dad knew Cassie didn't come to his office without a reason. His eyebrows went up. Way up. "Really?" he said. It sounded like a question.

I located an ancient Cheeto under a chair and crunched it down.

Cassie was quiet. Not answering. Then she started talking about something else — gardening. Gardening was another thing The Dad was good at. But I had no idea what it had to do with the case. And it wasn't the time for gardening. The days were getting colder and shorter. It was almost the time for snow. Not the season for digging in the dirt. Not for people anyway.

"So, if I wanted to fertilize plants, you know, for next year, is it too late?" Cassie asked. "Is it good to fertilize now, or only when you're putting in plants? And does fertilizer go bad? Like, expire?"

That was a lot of questions. I licked up stale popcorn crumbs while The Dad answered.

"Well, you could do some autumn topdressing in early November, you know, add fertilizer to the surface," The Dad said thoughtfully. "And I don't think fertilizer goes bad. It might lose some of the microbial benefits, but . . ."

"Is it dangerous for pets?" Cassie blurted, interrupting. "Like, if a dog ate a bunch of fertilizer, would it kill him?"

I sniffed a bit of hardened cheese out of a corner. *Mmmm.* Cheese.

The Dad nodded, like he suddenly understood. "I'd say if he got into it and ate enough, fertilizer could make him sick. But I don't think it would do Dodge any real harm."

I lifted my nose from the floor. The Dad scratched

my head, behind the ears. He thought we were talking about *me*!

"You been eating compost, Dodger?" he asked.

"Woof!" No! I would never. Ever. Well, maybe if it was really *good* compost. . . .

"Whew — that's good to hear!" Cassie changed the subject before I could fully defend myself. "So how are things going with Madame LeFarge?" she asked. Enough floor patrol. Now we were getting down to serious business.

The Dad perked up like a Yorkie with a mail carrier on his porch. "I'm not supposed to talk about a case before it's closed, but I think this one's pretty open and shut. You want to see?"

Cassie's mouth said "yes." But the rest of her body said *No way*. She did not like dead. But The Dad was so excited to show us that he didn't notice. He just led us to an examination room. It looked like the rooms at Pet Rescue, with metal tables and equipment. But bigger. Way bigger. And with drawers in the wall.

My nose went into overdrive. The drawers smelled like plastic, alcohol . . . and more. Even the cold drifting out of those drawers was pungent. The Dad pulled out a long one. There was a body inside. A body in a bag. I knew it was Madame before he unzipped it. She still smelled like herself. And like plastic, like cats, and like dead.

Cassie shrank back. She balled her fists and stuffed them in her pockets.

The Dad told her it was okay. He spoke gently. "It's science, honey. Biology."

Cassie nodded, but the look on her face said, *It's creepy, Dad. And gross!*

I gave The Dad's hand a lick to let him know I thought his job was cool. Even if Cassie didn't.

"You don't have to look." The Dad zipped Madame up and closed the drawer.

"Can you tell how she died?" Cassie asked.

"Blunt force trauma. I could see from the head wound that the impact was enough to kill her."

Cassie smelled rusty, like disappointment. That wasn't the answer she was hoping for. "So that's it? You're done with your investigation?"

The Dad nodded. "Open and shut."

"You're not going to check for poison, or alcohol in her blood stream, or anything?" Cassie prodded. She was like a dog with a bone, and she'd just started chewing. She wasn't giving up.

"Well, I've ordered a toxicology report, which checks for those things, as a matter of course. But I don't expect to find anything. She probably slipped and hit her head when she fell. Unfortunately, there was nobody there to help her. Only the cats."

Nobody there to help her. Hearing that made me think of Bananas. Back at the house, alone. The poor kid. I held back a whimper. I knew Cassie was still chewing, but I hoped we'd go soon.

"Hey, I'm almost out of here." The Dad looked at his wrist. "You guys want a ride home?"

Ride? I loved rides. Rides were my favorite. Wag, wag, wag. And a ride would get us home. Fast.

We waited, away from the drawer room, until it was time to leave. Then we rode. In The Dad's car. I got the whole backseat and hung my head out the window. My eyes closed. My ears flapped. My tongue lolled. What a way to forget the day. *Woof!* Everything smelled better at thirty miles per hour.

CHAPTER 16

I couldn't believe I'd seen a dead body up close. Or that it spooked me so bad. I knew every great detective had to do forensic research — dead people came with the job — but I really didn't have the stomach for it. On the drive home I wanted to stick my head out the window like Dodge. I thought maybe it would help with the barfiness. Luckily, the farther we got from Dad's office, the better I felt. Until we got home, at least.

The minute I opened the front door I could hear that something was wrong. Furball and Sam were both screeching at the top of their lungs. Upstairs, somewhere. So much for my recently settled stomach.

Dodge and I headed away from the noise and wound up in the kitchen, where Owen was trying to coax Bananas off the top of the fridge. He wasn't getting very far.

"What are you doing up there?" I asked while the kitten waved a claw at Owen.

Her head turned at the sound of my voice, and as soon as she spotted Dodge she hopped right down, using Owen's head as a step.

Owen clucked his tongue. "'Bananas' is right," he muttered. "She wouldn't even let me open the door to get the jam, but when *he* shows up . . ."

Bananas wove in and out of Dodge's legs, purring so loudly I could hear it over the yowls coming from upstairs. Not even Owen could keep from smiling.

Then Sam stormed into the kitchen, hissing and spitting like the cat in her arms. Bananas took one look at them and positioned herself safely between Dodge's four legs.

"That . . . that *thing* has got to go!" Sam shrieked, pointing at the kitten. "She attacked Furball and ripped her ear. There's blood all over my new bedspread!"

I scowled at Sam. I knew Bananas could be vicious, but Furball wasn't exactly a cream puff. Sam was just being super dramatic, as usual. She needed to cut the new cat a break. Bananas was an orphan!

Besides, I was mad at her for going into my room and snooping around — a crime I still hadn't nailed her for. Snooping was totally against family rules and there'd be a price to pay. I just wasn't sure what it was. While I seethed, Dodge just stood there, calmly protecting Bananas from further attacks. He wagged his tail and sidestepped, rolling over on his back and inviting Bananas to walk all over him. Like, literally.

The little cat accepted the invitation and strutted around on top of Dodge, sitting down once in a while like she'd brought the big dog down, pinned him, and was posing for victory shots. Dodge happily played along, letting her "win."

I was pretty sure my dog was trying to tell me something. So I decided to let Sam "win," too — at least for now. I couldn't find the energy to get into it with her, anyway. Then Dad came into the kitchen and Sam started whining to him.

"Daddy, she made poor Furball *bleed*," she whimpered. Furball mewed along pathetically, tucking her head. Her ears looked fine to me.

Dad got quiet for a second, then turned and looked me in the eye. His face was serious and I knew what he was going to say before he even opened his mouth. I nodded at phrases like "additional stress on the family" and "costly vet bills."

Wait, was Dad saying Bananas would have to leave? I stopped nodding and started arguing.

"Bananas is just adjusting to a new life," I said, trying to sound rational. "She won't be here forever."

"I know, honey. But if she can't get along with the pets we're committed to . . . the permanent members of our family . . ."

I looked at Dodge and Bananas on the floor, still tussling happily. The little cat was getting along just fine with *some* of the permanent family members. Dodge stopped playing long enough to give me a look of pure puppy concern. We couldn't let Bananas get booted out.

"Maybe we can just keep the cats separated for a little while." I tried not to sound beggy. "Until we can find Bananas her own family."

Dad looked at the furry pair on the kitchen floor, too, and relented, but barely. He didn't actually say Bananas could stay; he just didn't say she had to leave right that second. Which meant I had a new job to add to my list: find Bananas a home, quick! And while I was at it I could try to help the rest of Madame's cats, too.

After dinner Sam and Furball went upstairs while I cleaned up the kitchen and made a mental to-do list. On the top of the list: find out what Mom thought about the whole "slipped and fell" theory. A detective had to trust her instincts, and mine were screaming that something wasn't right. I needed to find out what Mom's were telling *her*.

It was a well-known fact in our family that Mom watched TV when she didn't want to think. So when I found her in front of the television watching a home makeover show I immediately wondered what she didn't want to think *about*. I knew better than to blurt out a bunch of questions, though. Mom had barely recovered from the stress of being suspended and was still dealing with the craziness of catching up at work. I was going to have to go in slow.

I gave Dodge a look he understood. He walked over and put his square head on Mom's knee, gazing up at her with his liquid chocolate eyes. She pet him limply, and Bananas (once she saw that this human was okay in Dodge's book) got close enough to attack Mom's shoelace.

Mom made room for me on the couch, and we both sat and stared at the screen. I wasn't sure what to say. Lucky for me Bananas wasn't afraid to speak up. She stopped thrashing the laces and let out a mew. It was so cute even Mom had to look.

"Oh, really?" She reached out a hand.

"I wouldn't do that if I were you," I warned. "She's kind of cranky. I think she misses Madame LeFarge."

Mom wisely pulled her hand back. "So does Henry Kales," she said with a wry smile.

My head turned. "Henry Kales?"

Mom nodded. "According to his niece Deb, he had a big crush on Laverne, but she wouldn't give him the time of day. At one point she even tried to file a restraining order against him."

Madame LeFarge's name was *Laverne*? No wonder she liked Madame. But that wasn't the only shocker. "What happened with that?" I asked. I pictured Henry on his porch across from Madame's house. Sitting and staring. It was definitely a little creepy, but was it threatening?

"Judge Thackery didn't buy it. Madame didn't have a lawyer, or any proof that Kales was a menace. All she had was a long history of calling the police about problems that weren't actually problems. So Thackery threw it out. It's funny that she took it so far. Kales was one of the few people who liked her. Oddly, he's not the only one who misses her. I do, too."

Now that was *really* hard to believe — even harder to believe than Erica Bloom missing Madame. "For real?" I asked.

"I know." Mom laughed softly. "It sounds ridiculous. Even to me. Would you believe I started to listen to the emergency report calls today, just in case . . . ?"

Dodge looked up at the sound of the word "case," and Mom shook the blanket fringe by the floor. Bananas pounced.

"Wait. Why would you be listening to emergency calls? It's not part of your job, is it?" This conversation was getting more baffling by the minute.

Mom shrugged. "As chief I'm responsible for making sure we handle calls correctly. The dispatcher downloads them daily so I can do random reviews and spot checks. I don't have time to listen every day, but they're on my computer — and until recently many of them were from Madame . . . when she didn't dial me direct."

"Right!" I snorted, remembering how much it bugged Mom that Madame repeatedly found her inside line.

"I never could figure out how she kept getting my number. Or why I didn't always change it when she did. I guess I kind of like eccentrics." She smiled halfheartedly.

Bananas grabbed Mom's shoelace, rolled on her back,

and "gutted" it with her hind legs as if it were a dangerous animal. I swear Dodge looked proud.

"I keep wondering if I should have paid more attention. But I just wasn't sure what to do with her," Mom said thoughtfully, gazing down at Bananas. "And now I'm not sure what to do with *you*!" she teased the little kitten.

I sucked in a big breath and let it all out, flapping my lips. *Pbbbbb.* I knew how she felt.

Upstairs, my posse and I settled on the floor. I had research to do and hoped my findings would lead me to my next step. I took out my notebook, the scrap from Erica Bloom's garbage, and the damaged bottle Dodge had given me. It was time to turn up my powers of observation.

The bottle had no label and no lid. It smelled like fish. I wrote that down. The white plastic was chewed, like a dog would chew a toy, only it was chewed by cats — smaller holes. That was strange. Cat toys were usually soft and moved so cats could chase them — like mice on strings. Or they had catnip in them. Were the cats trying to get something from inside the bottle? I wrote that down, too.

Next I smoothed out the scrap from the bag of fertilizer. I'd managed to get about half of the CAUTION label, but the plastic had stretched when I'd ripped it, messing up the printing. I could only read half of the ingredients.

Dodge put his head on my leg, his eyebrows twitching. "Yup," I agreed. "More info would have been nice."

I leaned back against my bed and tapped my pencil on the page. *Tap. Tap. Tap.* Tapping helped me think, and I needed to do some serious thinking. I had more questions than answers. I wrote those down, too:

1) Why would a gardener (Erica Bloom) throw away fertilizer?
   a. Was she trying to hide it?
   b. Was it lethal to cats? (Dad says probably not.)
   c. Was Erica trying to poison Madame's cats?

2) Why did Madame fall in her kitchen?
   a. Note: There were no bottles in recycling; she wasn't a drinker.
   b. No rugs/tripping hazards on the kitchen floor.

3) How does Henry Kales fit in?
   a. Stalker? Secret admirer?
   b. Since he was always watching (and said he found the body), could he have seen something?

c. If he was rejected, could he have *done* something?

d. Was Henry a threat?

I thought back to the last time I saw Madame alive. I closed my eyes and pictured Erica yelling her head off while Henry tried to help Madame to her feet. Madame had blown Henry off, but she didn't seem scared of him. Just annoyed. But if he wasn't a threat, why would she want a restraining order?

Oh, right. We were talking about Madame LeFarge. I pictured the double-parked truck, the minor traffic violation that Madame felt warranted a stakeout.

I sighed and gave Dodge a pat. I knew that a lot of what Madame complained about was blown out of proportion.

But what if all of it wasn't in her head?

CHAPTER 17

I was dozing on my bed with Bunny and The Kid. Or almost dozing. I couldn't actually sleep very well with the little cat curled up against me. I was afraid I might roll over and crush her. Plus, she purred like a lawn mower.

So I was somewhere between asleep and awake. Listening to the purr and Cassie's pencil scratching paper. Lying there, peaceful, when The Sister walked into our den.

"What do you want?" Cassie asked as soon as her pack mate stepped into our territory. She didn't look up. Didn't make eye contact. The sisters were on the outs. Mostly it was about the felines. But something else, too. Something to do with the day we got in trouble for being on Prospect Street. When The Sister's scent was all over our den.

"I just came to tell you something," The Sister said in a pouty voice.

"'Kay. What?" Cassie still didn't look up.

"Summer stopped by before dinner. While you were at Dad's office."

Summer? My good ear stood a little taller.

Cassie's lip twitched. She kept her head down, but her heartbeat picked up speed. Summer always made Cassie's hackles rise. And her coming by was definitely suspect. "Did she throw rocks at my window?" Cassie asked, almost showing her teeth.

The Sister stepped back. "I don't know why you're so mean to her," she said. Still pouty. She stared at her feet. Disappointed. "She's nice," she added more softly.

Cassie jerked her head up. She looked The Sister in the eyes. Held them — a challenge. "Nice? Are you kidding?"

"Yeah. Nice." The Sister said, staring back. She even raised her chin a little. The sharp smell of a fight made my nostrils twitch. "There must be something you like about her. You used to be best friends."

Cassie cringed. I cocked my head one way, then the other. *What?* My girl used to be friends with Summer? *Best* friends? That wasn't possible. Hayley was Cassie's best friend. Well, human friend. Right after me. I figured The

Sister was just clawing at scraps to get back at Cassie for what The Kid had done to The Cat. Or maybe my good ear was going bad.

"Get out," Cassie barked. She wasn't fooling, either. She was ferocious. The Sister had found a tender spot, a spot Cassie was protecting.

The Sister rolled her eyes and turned on her sparkly heel. "Whatever," she said, and walked away.

That night Cassie brushed her teeth extra hard before coming to bed. She hurled her clothes into the basket. And she didn't fall asleep quickly. She sighed. And tossed. And turned. And sighed.

I listened. And chewed. The Kid was the only one in our den getting any rest.

Cassie was stewing on the Madame situation. And the Bananas situation. And the Summer situation, which was the weirdest situation of all. How could she have such a sore spot — the kind that made her show her teeth — that I didn't know about?

After a long time Cassie gave up on sleeping. She got up and started working at her desk. She scratched on paper. She tapped on the computer. Then she aimed her phone at The Kid, who was asleep on my back. Cassie took a picture, then tapped some more. Finally she padded downstairs to the office. I would have followed, but The Kid was having a dream, and it seemed like a good one.

When Cassie got back she showed me a paper. It had a lot of squiggles on it. And a picture of Bananas.

"That ought to do the trick," she said.

Trick? What trick? Cassie didn't explain, but I think it worked. She fell into bed, yawned once, and was asleep. *Woof.* Good trick.

CHAPTER 18

Alicia and Hayley came over after school to help me finish up the flyers. I felt a tiny bit guilty because I was supposed to be at Pet Rescue, but when I told Gwen my plan she told me that finding homes for the cats was top priority; she could do the afternoon chores without me. And I had to admit that the flyer had turned out great — especially the picture of Bananas, the resident cutie. I couldn't wait to get them up.

"She's so adorable!" Alicia said as she watched Bananas and Dodge wrestle. Hugo, her rescued rottweiler, stared in amazement. He clearly had no idea what to make of the fearless kitten.

"Totally adorable," Hayley agreed. "But do you think she might be part dog?"

"Meowf!" Bananas interjected.

I smirked and tossed Dad's staple gun into my back-pack along with a roll of packing tape. "Dodge seems to think so," I said. "I'm pretty sure she likes his kibble, too."

Laughing, the six of us trooped to the copy shop. I momentarily considered telling my friends about the dream I'd been having — the one with me standing at the bottom of the tree fort, betrayed. But dreaming about Summer was bad enough; I didn't really want to talk about her when I was awake. And Hayley had heard all the details, anyway. She knew how Summer and I became friends in preschool and how our friendship crashed and burned in fourth grade.

Lucky for me, Hayley moved to Bellport the summer that Summer turned horrible. Hayley even had a good-turned-evil best friend of her own at her old school. She didn't want to think about Ashley any more than I wanted to think about Summer. So we decided to act like it had always just been us, like those brat girls had never existed. It was silly, but it worked. At least until now.

"Hey, Mr. Karahi," I greeted when we piled through the copy shop door. Mr. Karahi had two dogs of his own that he'd adopted from PR a few years ago, and welcomed canines in his crowded store. "We need to make about a hundred flyers."

He gazed at the picture of Bananas on the paper in my hand. "Nice kitty."

"Meowf!" the actual Bananas replied.

Mr. Karahi blinked in surprise. He hadn't seen Bananas on Dodge's back.

"She's one of Madame LeFarge's," Hayley explained.

Mr. Karahi's face darkened. "So sad," he said. Then he sort of shook his head and directed us to a copy machine. "This one is best today. The others are jamming like crazy."

I nodded and set my flyer on the glass, then pushed buttons. A few minutes later we had one hundred and one flyers ready to go.

Mr. Karahi wouldn't let me pay. "On the house, Cassie," he insisted. "Always happy to help Pet Rescue. Do you have everything you need to put them up?"

I nodded and showed him my tape and staple gun. "Excellent," he said. "Good luck."

"Thank you!" Alicia called as we headed out. We left the edge of downtown and turned onto Chestnut, putting up posters as we went.

"If I didn't already have Hugo, I'd totally want Bananas," Alicia declared as I stapled a poster to a telephone pole. Hugo was a former Pet Rescue dog. He'd had a cruel first owner, but was a happy boy in his new life.

Hearing his name, he glanced up from the fire hydrant he was sniffing and let out a bark.

"Meowf!" Bananas replied from Dodge's back. The tiny tiger had no fear of dogs — any dogs. She was totally one of the pack.

"That is one crazy, adorable kitty-dog," Hayley announced. "Or doggie-cat."

We passed a bunch of county buildings, and even in the daylight the gray stone reminded me of my visit to Dad's office. I shuddered. I could still picture Madame LeFarge's dead body. Plus, Dad's assessment was still bugging me. Toxicology reports took a really long time, and I was impatient. There *had* to be something in there.

"I still think it's weird that Madame LeFarge just fell down and died," Hayley said, studying my face. She knew what I was thinking.

I nodded my agreement and stapled a flyer with extra oomph. "Totally."

"Do you think she was drugged?" she continued, her dark eyes widening. "Or pushed?"

"I do think something made her fall," I said.

"That sounds awful." Alicia looked alarmed.

"Awfully suspicious," Hayley said in a low voice. She loved a murder.

When we got to Madame's street we hung extra flyers and stuck them under doormats. Henry was in his usual spot on his porch, sitting and staring.

"I'll be right back," I told my friends. I put on a friendly, innocent face and walked toward Henry with Dodge and his passenger at my side. Henry did so much watching I thought maybe he'd seen something useful. As we approached, though, I wasn't so sure. He was staring at Madame's house so intently he didn't even see us. I thought maybe we were invisible when he started and turned, narrowing his eyes.

"What do you want?" he asked gruffly.

I smiled and handed him a flyer. "We're trying to find homes for Madame LeFarge's cats. There were thirteen of them, and —"

"I know precisely how many there were," he interrupted. "She loved those animals like they were her own children. They were her entire world." He bit down on the last two words, then crumpled the flyer into a ball and dropped it to the ground. "If you ask me they don't *deserve* homes!"

Wow. He was mad. I flashed to my list, mentally highlighting "rejected." An admirer who'd been turned down could do really bad things. Only they usually tried to hide their rage, at least a little. . . . "Oh, well, sorry to bother you," I offered, backing away.

"What was that about?" Alicia asked when we reached the sidewalk.

"I'm not completely sure, but he definitely won't be adopting any cats."

Hayley nodded. "That seemed obvious." She led the way across the street, right to Bill Heinz's door. "May as well interview the other mysterious neighbor," she said, ringing the bell.

The six of us stood on Bill's porch, waiting. Finally we heard footsteps, and the door opened. Bill's sparse hair was standing straight up, but he smiled at us.

"Whoa, it's a porch party," he said in a friendly way. It smelled like he was frying fish in the kitchen, and the dogs' noses started twitching like crazy.

"Hi, I'm Cassie Sullivan, and these are my friends, human, canine, and feline," I said, handing him a flyer.

"Woof!" Hugo punctuated.

"We're trying to find homes for Madame LeFarge's thirteen cats. Do you think you might be interested in adopting one?"

"A couple of her cats live here already," he said with a dry laugh.

That stopped me. "Really?" I asked, needing more information.

"Well, not really," he said, glancing at the flyer. "They just come around sometimes. You know cats, always prowling."

I knew. Furball was a sly one.

"But, seriously, I'll think about it. And I'd invite you all in but I'm sort of in the middle of a project."

"A fish and chips project?" Hayley asked, her nose wrinkling.

Bill looked surprised for a second, then nodded. "Uh, yeah. Exactly," he confirmed. "I've actually got fish cooking right now, so if you'll excuse me . . ." He retreated into his house, closing the door.

"He's way friendlier than the other guy," Alicia remarked after the door clicked shut, and I was surprised to agree. I could actually see what Erica meant by "good neighbor."

I pondered these new details as we paraded back to the sidewalk. Then, out of the blue, a new idea popped into my head. "Let's take some flyers over to Home Away from Home."

"Ooh, that's good. I bet some of the residents have grandchildren who'd love a kitten," Hayley agreed.

"Exactly." I was nodding when my phone chimed. I pulled it out and stared.

BornBlonde: Meet me @ Roberts Park, tom 4:30.

BornBlonde was Summer. As in Summer Hill.

Clued-In: Um. Wrong number?
BornBlonde: I'm serious.
Clued-In: What's up?
BornBlonde: Tell u there.

Huh? I didn't know what to think. I *couldn't* think. I just stood there like a big dummy.

"Who was that? Did something happen?" Alicia asked, noticing my paralysis. Hayley looked concerned and Dodge nudged my knee.

I dropped the phone to my side and the bomb on my friends. "That was Summer. She wants to meet with me."

CHAPTER 19

I nudged Cassie behind the knees to get her to stop staring at her phone. To get her moving. I'd heard her say Home Away from Home, and I was excited. All that postering had made me hungry. Hungry for Peanut Butter Buddies. Plus I loved the old-timers. And Peanut Butter Buddies.

But Cassie wasn't moving, and neither was Alicia. Or Hayley. "You can't be serious," she said.

Cassie handed Hayley her phone. "Dead serious."

Woof. What did I miss?

Hayley stared at the phone, her mouth hanging open in a very un-Hayley way. "That's just crazy."

"No kidding," Cassie agreed. "As crazy as Madame LeFarge. Maybe crazier."

"Woof!" I barked out loud this time, to get everyone moving. I wasn't sure what they were talking about, but I was ready to go. Go! Hugo was, too. We bounded ahead and I felt Bananas sink her claws into my fur. Good thing I liked The Kid.

Stopping to turn back, I panted with relief. They were finally coming, and Cassie's phone was nowhere in sight.

Cassie pulled open the door for us and I trotted into Home Away. Esther and Paul were in the front room. Their faces smiled at us, but I smelled their sad. They looked worried under their smiles, too. Like they'd been skunked. Esther was wringing her soft hands. And someone was missing.

"Where's Duke?" Cassie asked, scanning the room. "Out training for a marathon?"

Nobody laughed at her joke, and Cassie's face shifted. She couldn't smell the sad like I could, but she was starting to feel it. She knew something was wrong.

Esther shook her head. "Duke collapsed yesterday," she said. "He's in the hospital. We're still waiting for news."

CHAPTER 20

"That's awful!" I said, unable to believe it. The day was taking another bad turn. Duke MacLean didn't belong in the hospital — the last time I saw him he was doing chin-ups! "What happened?"

Esther shook her head. "We weren't with him," she explained, "but one of the nurses said he was walking down the hallway and fell. Collapsed, just like that." Her eyes welled up. I gave her a hug, and Dodge licked Paul's hand. Bananas was surprisingly still and quiet. I wanted to tell Esther that he'd be fine, as good as new in no time. But what if it wasn't true? What if he . . . ?

I squeezed my eyes shut. This was hitting me hard. I suddenly wanted to see Duke, to go straight to the hospital. But how could I do that? I wasn't a relative, and

I was with a pack of friends, fur-covered and otherwise. Not exactly discreet.

No. My visit to Duke would have to be planned carefully. It would have to wait.

"We just have to be patient," Paul said, putting a shaky hand on Esther's shoulder. "They'll call as soon as they know something."

I nodded, glad that Esther and Paul didn't have to wait for news about their friend alone. We visited for a while, and gave them some flyers. "We'll be sure to tell everyone about them," Esther said, her eyes bright. "I'm sure someone here knows someone who would love a fuzzy friend."

"Meowf!" Bananas agreed.

I gently squeezed Esther's hand. "Thank you. That would be a huge help."

She sniffled and smiled, and we said good-bye. "Dodge and I will be back in a few days," I promised.

"I'm sure we'll have news by then," Esther said.

Outside, we gathered on the sidewalk. "Holy cow," Alicia said. "They must be scared to death."

"I'm glad they have each other, at least." I pulled out my phone to call Gwen and let her know about our progress. If nothing else, we'd successfully spread the word about Madame's cats. I hit speed dial and listened as the call rang through.

"Pet Rescue," Gwen answered. But it wasn't her cheerful, capable phone voice. She sounded upset.

"Hi, Gwen, it's me, Cassie. What's wrong?"

Gwen sighed heavily on the other end of the line, and I braced myself. Gwen was *not* a sigher. "That obvious?" she asked sadly. "Oh, Cassie. Salt and Pepper died this morning."

"Oh, no!" I suddenly felt woozy, like I'd been kicked in the stomach. This was terrible — the worst news I'd heard all day. And I'd been getting plenty of bad news.

"The other sick cats don't seem to be getting worse, so that's good," she said. "But when Pepper died I . . ." Her voice caught, and she let out a ragged exhale.

"Oh, Gwen, I'm so sorry. That must have been horrible." Hayley and Alicia were watching me with big worried eyes.

"It's just so — I don't understand it," Gwen said. "They were cared for in a good home. It's not like they came in off the streets."

"Do we know what they died of?"

"We're not sure, but Dr. Byrnes is going to do a postmortem to see if she can figure it out. It's weird, though."

Definitely, I thought. The cats hadn't been old. My mind flashed to the bag in Erica's trash, and then to Madame's claims about poison. Crazy fantasy or crazy fact? Anything was possible, and one thing was certain: I still had more research to do.

"I have a small bit of good news," I told her. "We put adoption flyers up all over town, and even have a few leads."

"Well, that's something," Gwen said, sounding a little better. "Thanks, Cassie, and to your friends, too. You're a big help."

I felt like anything but. Two kitties had died, and I couldn't do a thing about it. I hung up the phone, feeling deflated. "Only eleven cats to find homes for now," I told my friends. "We lost two this morning." I glanced at Bananas, hoping she didn't understand what I'd just said.

We walked back to my house in silence, thinking about poor Salt and Pepper, and poor Duke. Dodge's tail hung low between his legs. Even Bananas seemed defeated.

"Call me later if you need anything," Hayley said. "Or better yet, I'll call you." She gave me a hug, and Alicia wrapped her arms around both of us.

"Thanks, guys," I said.

"Whuff!" Dodge agreed as we started up the walk. But he didn't sound like his energetic self.

Inside and upstairs, I snatched the laptop from Sam's room. I searched for "cat poisons," and a list of the top-ten household poisons for pets popped up. Among them were human medications, certain kinds of people food, rat poison, and fertilizer. Fertilizer! There was definitely more than one way to kill a cat. . . .

CHAPTER 21

The biggest bummer about being a twelve-year-old detective was — you guessed it — school. Having to be at Harbor Middle for thirty-two-plus hours a week totally got in the way of my sleuthing. I mean 8:30 to 3:00? That was practically the whole day! I could ditch, of course. Only my mom was chief of police, and they took truancy pretty seriously in Bellport. Plus I actually cared — more than I wanted to admit — about my classes. So I saved skipping for serious emergencies.

Also, I had other important stuff to keep tabs on. Like Summer Hill. The wave of bad news had distracted me from Summer's freaky behavior, but hadn't made it go away. I had to keep an eye on that girl without letting her know I was watching. She was up to something and I wanted to know what it was *before* I walked into an ambush. Like the one she clearly had planned for me at Roberts Park. I was racking my brain to figure out why in the world she would want me to meet her — and trying to get a clue from her behavior.

I managed to keep my surveillance on the down low all morning. But then, at lunch, I let my guard down and she caught me looking right at her. Again! And ugh! She *smiled* in my direction. Again!

"That is totally creepy," Hayley said as I winced and turned away. It was, too. Summer was probably the only person I knew who could smile without seeming the slightest bit nice, or even happy.

Meanwhile, Summer's blondetourage was missing. *Probably up a tree, laughing about my detective "hobby,"* I thought grimly.

Hayley handed me a piece of homemade toffee. "I made this for you last night. Thought you might need something sweet."

"Do I ever," I said, biting into the nutty goodness. "Especially when dealing with the Queen of Mean over there."

Alicia reached for her own piece of toffee. "Are you going to meet her today?"

The twenty-million-dollar question. "I don't know," I said slowly. I was trying to savor the buttery caramel flavor bursting in my mouth, but having Summer in my line of sight was adding a decided hint of bitterness. "I really want to go see Duke in the hospital, but I told Gwen I'd come to Pet Rescue. She's still really upset about Salt and Pepper. And worried about the other cats who are sick."

Alicia shook her head. "Losing two cats must feel terrible. I mean, *I* feel terrible, and I never even met them. It's just so sad!" She was quiet for a long moment, then sat up straighter. "Maybe I could go to Pet Rescue for you. I'd love to help in some way."

I shook my head. If only! "That's totally nice of you, but you'd have to complete volunteer training before you could sub for me. There are all kinds of rules about caring for animals in shelters." My fingers drummed on the tabletop. "But I'm pretty sure you could come *with* me to help," I added.

Alicia's whole face lit up. "Really? I could?"

"Me, too?" Hayley wanted in.

"You're both on," I said, feeling myself smile for the first time all day.

After school the three of us headed straight to PR. Gwen gave me a grateful smile when she saw me, but she looked totally fried. "I never thought I'd say this, but I'm glad you didn't bring Dodge." She wheeled her chair back to show me one of the cats asleep on her lap — a big gray male. "You know I love your dog, but I think he'd upset the kitties. They're having a hard enough time as it is."

I nodded knowingly and gave the cat a gentle scratch under the chin. "Who's this again?"

"Parsley. He's so upset about his siblings that he cries whenever he's not being held." Her eyes were full of worry. "Dr. Byrnes didn't find anything poisonous in Pepper or Salt, but she noticed some elevated levels in their blood work. She's testing the sick cats now."

The unsolved mysteries were making my head spin. Madame LeFarge's death. Summer's message. Duke getting sick. Cats dying. The weird stuff just kept piling up! "What was elevated?" I barely remembered to ask. The online list of poisons were still in my head, and I wondered how fertilizer would show up in a blood panel. I remembered a poster about plants from science class, about the nutrients they needed to grow. Nitrogen was at the top of the list. Maybe it would show up as nitrogen.

"That's the weird thing," Gwen said. "It was just elevated vitamin levels. Nothing toxic."

Hmmm. Interesting.

We helped Gwen feed the cats, then walked the dogs. A few of them weren't leash trained, and kept getting tangled up. It took forever even though there were three of us (or maybe *because* there were three of us!). By the time we finished it was 4:25, and I was feeling totally torn. I wanted to see Duke. I wanted to get Dodge. And deep down I knew that I *had* to meet Summer. Ugh. Just the thought of seeing her made me cringe.

"Cassie, it's going to be okay." Hayley could read me like a book.

"I'd like to believe you," I said with a huge sigh.

"You're going to meet Summer, right? I really think —"

"Maybe *you* should go meet Summer," I grumbled. The whole situation was making me whiny.

Hayley smiled. "I would if I thought it would help. But if you don't —"

I held up a hand. "I know, I know. If I don't get to the bottom of Summer's bizarre behavior, it will get weirder."

"And drive you crazier," Alicia put in.

They were both right, of course. And I knew it. I swung a leg over my bike and pushed off before I could change my mind. "Okay, I'm going," I said grimly as I rolled down the sidewalk. "I'll call you later."

I pedaled slowly, thinking. I was late and it would be faster to go straight to Roberts Park without getting Dodge.

But no Dodge? No way.

If I was going to face Summer Hill, I was definitely going to need Dodge by my side.

CHAPTER 22

I could tell Cassie was coming. I could always tell when Cassie was coming. What I *couldn't* tell was that she was in a hurry. And anxious. I had to wait for her to be within sniffing distance for that.

She threw open the front door without saying anything, and I followed her out. She smelled like cider vinegar and a hint of bacon. Always bacon. Her mouth stayed in a flat line. She moved fast. Her body was tense. So tense I couldn't even enjoy the wind in my fur.

I didn't know where we were going, either. I usually did, but today I didn't. So I ran a few paces behind. Yeah, I let Cassie lead. She turned her bike toward the hills, away from the ocean. I followed.

She pedaled hard up a steep hill.

"Woof!" I barked happily. I knew where we were going now! To Roberts Park. Roberts Park was big and open. It had grass. Picnic leftovers. Squirrels. It had dirt to dig. So much to sniff!

But as we got close I smelled things that didn't belong in a park. Nail polish. Lip gloss. Bubble bath. *Woof,* what? Those weren't the smells of Roberts Park. Those things smelled like . . . Summer.

Cassie was leading us to Summer? My nose knew first. My eyes confirmed. I saw Summer's light hair. I saw Muffet's light fur.

Muffet! I trotted forward to greet the little dog, then stopped. *Woof!* What?

Thanks to her owner, Muffet often wore ridiculous outfits. Ruffles. Fringe. Froof. It was weird, but I was used to it. Only this was extreme. Muffet had on a ballet tutu, complete with satin slippers that laced up her legs. I could barely look.

Lucky for her, the Maltese didn't seem to mind. She hopped off Summer's lap. She yipped and wagged. She twirled like a tiny ballerina. Then she tried to get a whiff of what I'd been up to. I expected Summer to freak, but she didn't. She let Muffet do her dog thing. And I did mine. *Sniff, sniff, sniff.*

I was busy making sure Muffet still smelled like dog under all that perfume. So busy that I forgot to pay attention to my girl. Then she started to talk, and I remembered. Her sharp tone told me I had a job to do. She was upset. She needed backup. I stopped sniffing and moved in close.

"Where'd you get that? It's mine," Cassie howled. She pointed, too. At a book in Summer's hands. Not the kind Cassie got at the library. No. The kind people glued pictures into.

"It's *ours*," Summer corrected. Her face scrunched up and she pulled the book closer. "We made it together, remember?"

Cassie folded her arms over her stomach. Protected her guts. Good instincts. "Riiight. And then you threw it into the garbage and *I* fished it out. I'm pretty sure that's when you lost ownership."

Summer stared, and I moved even closer to Cassie. *Woof.* It was a standoff. How could these two have been friends? The only thing I smelled between them was the waxy scent of distrust.

Summer shifted from one foot to the other. Nervous. "Well, if you didn't want — well, then why did you leave it on my doorstep?" she asked. Her face was squinched together in a weird way.

Cassie stepped back fast, like she'd run into an electric fence. "I didn't! Why would I?" Then, slowly, she squinted back at Summer, nodding. She'd figured something out. "Sam," she whispered, almost silently. Her paws balled into fists. She wasn't confused anymore. She was mad. Really mad. And not at Summer, either.

"Woof!" I barked, but she ignored me.

"*Sam!*" she muttered again.

This was not good.

CHAPTER 23

I stood in front of Summer feeling like a complete idiot. I'd been tricked. Summer and I had both been tricked. She'd found the scrapbook on her doorstep? Only one person could have made that happen: my obnoxious little sister. Sam must have swiped the scrapbook from my room last week. The meddling snoop went into my room and stole it. I was going to *kill* her!

It definitely wasn't news to me that Sam adored Summer. They were both fashion obsessed. They were both way into glitter. They both thought being popular was *super* important. Back when Summer and I were friends, my little sister followed her around like a tiny clone. Sam was devastated when we had our huge fight. She spent a whole year trying to get us to be friends again.

Apparently she was *still* trying to get us to be friends. As if! I couldn't remember what I *ever* liked about Summer Hill — even when I tried really, really hard.

"I didn't leave it," I told Summer honestly through gritted teeth.

Summer's face was like the sky on a stormy day — it kept changing. First she looked puzzled, like I didn't make any sense. Then, for just a second, she looked sad. Finally her usual snotty Summer expression blew in, and stayed.

"I'm so glad," she snapped. "Because the only thing dumber than this dumb book is the fact that we were ever friends." She made a big show of dropping the scrapbook, which fell open to the page marked "Sleuthing Secrets." I gulped while Summer snatched up Muffet and ground her foot onto the picture of us holding my first detective notebook. As if she hadn't already made her point.

"Rowf!" Dodge let out a sharp bark as Summer stomped to her bike.

I patted his flank. "No kidding," I told him, glad that one of us had come up with a retort. "But at least she's leaving." Memories and nightmares — all involving Summer — swirled in my mind. I shook my head like

Dodge did when he had something in his ear, but the dreadful images didn't go anywhere. They were stuck.

The scrapbook wasn't going anywhere, either. It lay there, staring up at me like roadkill. I glanced down at the open page, at the picture of Summer and me with our goofy smiles and invisible-ink pens. We actually did have fun together, once upon a time. It seemed unbelievable now, even though I knew it was true. Maybe because everything changed the second Summer shared our book — and my dreams — with Celeste and Eva. They'd made fun of my sleuthing notes, laughing right in my face. But the worst part was Summer laughing with them, pretending she hated our spying, telling them it was a joke.

"She thinks she's Sherlock Holmes!" She'd cackled behind her hand. "You wouldn't believe the stupid crime stories she makes up!"

I bent and picked up the scrapbook, running a finger over the picture. I tried to rub off the print of Summer's shoe, but it was permanent. Just like our history.

I was really mad when Summer let Eva and Celeste into our fort without asking, when she showed them the book. But when they laughed and said those cruel things, I was more than mad. I was hurt.

Cut.

Crushed.

It made me realize that Summer wasn't a real friend. That she could never be a real friend. I was tempted to rip the picture out of the book — or at least Summer's half. I wanted to erase her altogether. But that, of course, was impossible.

Dodge whimpered, and I stroked his soft fur. Unlike Summer, Dodge knew how to be a friend. He hurt when I hurt, and vice versa. That's what friends did; they felt for each other. But *that* required feelings, which Summer totally lacked. "Thanks, boy," I told him, whispering into his soft ear. "I can always count on you."

CHAPTER 24

assie carried the big book over to a trash can, and I followed. She smelled sad, like a wilted rose. My nose quivered as she held the book over the garbage. She wanted to throw it away. It made her eyes shiny. I'd seen it before — books that upset humans. And this was a big one.

But Cassie didn't let go of the book. She just held it in the air, trying to make her paw drop it in the can. Standing this close to the trash, my nose went into overdrive. There was stuff in that can that I wanted to get *out*. Like a bit of roast beef sandwich. Maybe a big bit. Cassie didn't smell the sandwich — her nose was practically useless. Plus she was distracted.

I watched and waited. And, okay, drooled. A little. Finally Cassie let out a big sigh and carried the book back to the bench. She didn't drop it in the can. She didn't get anything out of the can, either.

I think I whimpered. I didn't like to see her so upset. And I didn't like to waste food. Especially roast beef! I licked my chops.

"Ugh," Cassie said, opening the book. She started at the beginning and went page by page. I rested my head on her knee and tried not to think about sandwiches. Cassie scratched behind my ears. I could smell her feelings. There were a lot of them mixed up together. Happy. Sad. Mad. It smelled like old mud. She laughed twice — a regular laugh and a strange one I didn't understand.

Pages turned. My chin stayed put. Cassie sighed. The sad faded a little, but the mad stayed. Finally she got to her feet and shoved the book into her backpack. "Enough is enough," she said. "Let's go, Dodge." She sounded a little tired, but also determined. *Woof!* That's right! Head up, Cassie!

I trotted next to her the whole way down the hill, enjoying the wind in my ears. Thinking about dinner. It wouldn't be roast beef, but it would be food. Yeah. Food. I loved food. Food was my favorite.

The closer we got to the house, the harder Cassie pedaled. By the time we turned onto Salisbury Drive I didn't smell any happy or sad anymore. The mad had taken over.

My girl's face was tight. Her mouth was a straight line. She was snarling angry, and it didn't take a trained K-9 to know why. The Sister had dug up something she shouldn't have. Something Cassie'd buried a long time ago. Something that was supposed to *stay* buried. Forever.

Cassie rolled up the driveway and skidded to a halt. She hopped off her bike, dropped it in the yard, and pounded up the walk. She threw open the door and yelled, loud. "Samantha Sullivan, where are you?"

The Sister looked up from the living room couch only a few feet away. Cassie yanked the scrapbook out of her backpack and stuck it under The Sister's nose. "This is *mine*!" she growled. "Mine!"

The Sister didn't say anything. She just stared. Wide-eyed but not innocent.

"You stole it from my room! You gave it to Summer and let her think it was from me!"

The Sister sat frozen. The only parts of her that moved were her eyelids, which blinked fast. If she were a dog,

133

she'd have been on the ground. Belly up, begging for mercy. "I — I —" she stammered.

"You what?" Cassie was madder than I'd ever seen her. I took a step back. I ignored my urges to retreat into a corner, or join her in the fight.

The Sister had a hard time getting the words out. "I . . . I just thought that maybe you two —"

Cassie leaned over The Sister. "Summer and I are *none of your business*!" she howled. "None!"

I heard footsteps behind me and turned. The Brother was there. He'd heard the fight and come out of his den to see what was going on. He glanced from one flushed face to the other. He paused. He knew it was dangerous to get between tangling sisters.

Finally he opened his mouth. "You went into Cassie's room without asking?" he asked in his rumbly voice. "And gave her stuff to someone else?"

The Sister shrank into the couch a little. She looked like a cornered chipmunk. Like she wanted to dig a hole and hide in it.

Cassie's lip was still curled but The Brother's backup smoothed her fur. I saw her paws uncurl a little, too. She took a breath and her phone chimed.

She pulled it out of her pocket and stared at the screen for a long time. The room was silent. Finally she looked back at The Sister. "Stay out of my room, and out of my personal life," she growled. "Or else."

The Brother nodded.

Pack justice.

CHAPTER 25

My blood was still pounding as Dodge and I headed into the kitchen. Lighting into my sister made me feel better, as did Owen's unexpected weigh-in. But it would take a little while for me to fully calm down. I squinted at my cell phone, trying to breathe and reread the message on my screen.

TopCop: Hey Sweetie. Working late tonight to catch up on filing. ☹ I'll be home to say good night. ☺

Mom almost never missed dinner, so this was unusual. But her message had given me an idea. The first part of which was getting dinner — make-your-own burritos — made.

"Meowf!" Bananas called from her perch on top of the fridge, and I felt a little bad. If I hadn't been screaming my head off at Samantha, she'd be down already.

"Sorry, Nanners," I told her sheepishly. She didn't seem too upset as she hopped onto my head, then to the floor to wrestle with Dodge. They really were an unlikely but irresistible pair. I watched their routine and felt my anger and sadness melt away, leaving me exhausted.

I pulled a can of pinto beans out of the cupboard and chopped some onion and garlic. The kitchen was just starting to smell good when Owen walked in.

"Want any help?" he asked.

I blinked in surprise. Owen was not exactly the type to volunteer for stuff. Especially lately.

"I'm good," I replied. "It's burritos — easy."

"Mom's on a Mexican food kick, huh?" he remarked. He pulled out a bag of rice and measured water into a pot. It wasn't his night to be on prep, but it was nice to be in the kitchen together.

"Thanks for chiming in out there," I said, gesturing toward the living room with my chin.

He shook his head. "No problem. She crossed a line for sure."

My plan for the evening flashed in my head, and I wondered if *I* was crossing a line. But I couldn't falter. I had a case to solve.

As soon as the ingredients were ready I made a burrito for Mom, wrapped it in foil, and shoved it into a paper bag with a napkin. "Tell Dad that I'm delivering Mom's dinner to the station. You guys should start without me."

Owen nodded a little. "Will do."

I walked into the hall and shoved the burrito into my backpack, ignoring Sam. Dodge and Bananas waited patiently at the door. When I opened it they raced down the walk. Fifteen minutes later we poked our heads into Mom's office.

"Dinner delivery," I announced with a grin.

Mom looked up, surprised. "Oh, Cassie, thank you." She rubbed her temples. "I didn't get lunch today, and I think my eyes might be permanently crossed."

I shook my head as Dodge and Bananas ambled forward to greet her.

"Maybe you should take a quick walk around the block — give yourself a little breather," I suggested as casually as I could. "I double wrapped the burrito, so it'll stay warm. I could even do a little filing while you're gone."

"Woof!" Dodge agreed, pawing the industrial carpet lightly. Mom nodded and pushed her chair back all at once. "That sounds great," she admitted. "I'll take the dynamic duo with me."

"Cool. They'd love it. They've been cooped up most of the day."

I silently told Dodge to keep her outside as long as possible.

"We'll be back in ten, all right?" Mom said.

I wanted to tell her to take her time, but that would've made her suspicious. Mom was smart like that. "Sounds good," I said instead. Ten minutes wasn't very long, but it would have to be enough.

As soon as Dodge's tail disappeared out the door I plunked myself down in Mom's chair. I was about to wake her computer when something on her desk caught my eye. A copy of a restraining order, with Henry Kales's name on it. Wait, hadn't Mom said that Judge Thackery threw out Madame's request? I scanned the paper, searching for the name of the person who filed it. Luella Swan, not Laverne LeFarge. This was a second restraining order, which made Henry Kales seem creepier than ever.

My brain churned and I turned my attention to the computer. The clock was ticking! I wasn't super familiar with the system, but had prowled around on it before. This time, though, I was searching for something specific. Something I could download and listen to. Miraculously, it was right there on the desktop — a folder labeled "Incident Report Audio." My heart started to beat wildly. I plugged in my iPod and dragged the files onto the icon. The words "copying 2,138 files" popped up on the screen, and I gulped. That was a lot! I stared at the blue progress bar, willing the files to copy quickly. Mom's desk clock ticked. The bar moved slowly. Too slowly!

I was sorting the papers in Mom's file pile and trying not to sweat when I heard the station door open. Eight hundred forty-two files to go. I was going to have to abort the download! Luckily Dodge caught whatever panic vibes I was emitting and kept the distraction going. He trotted over to the dog dish by the water cooler and gave a low woof.

The progress bar kept moving. . . .

"Empty?" Mom asked, walking over to fill it up.

"Come on!" I murmured under my breath. My heart thudded so hard I thought it was going to burst out of my chest.

The upload finished and I yanked my USB out of the port. I shoved the cord into my pocket just as Mom strolled into the office. "Nice walk?" I asked, smiling broadly. I hoped I didn't sound out of breath.

Mom smiled. "Lovely," she said. "And I can't wait for that burrito."

CHAPTER 26

When we got home, Dad, Owen, and Sam were still at the table. I knew I needed to eat (and couldn't get out of dinner anyway), but the files I'd just downloaded were a serious distraction. All I wanted to do was listen for clues. Dodge, though, went right to his bowl. I scooped him and Bananas some kibble, then took my seat in the dining room.

I took a bite of burrito and chewed listlessly while Sam eyed me from across the table. "How are things at Pet Rescue?" she asked in a teensy voice I barely recognized.

I squinted at her in confusion. Then I got it. She was trying to apologize for her major felony by acting interested in my life. I was seriously tempted to let her squirm, but she looked sort of washed out — her sparkle wasn't sparkling. For some weird reason I didn't feel happy about that, so I let her off the hook.

"It's kinda sad, actually," I answered honestly. "Two of Madame's cats died, and a couple more are still sick. It makes it harder than usual to find homes, and we need ten of them."

"Meowf!" Bananas said plaintively, coming into the dining room and slipping under the table with Dodge.

"Right. Make that eleven."

Owen and Dad both set their burritos down, and Dad reached over to squeeze my arm. Sam stared at me with wide eyes.

"I wish Furball and Bananas could be friends," Sam said sadly. "Or at least be friendly to each other."

I eyed my limp little sister and wondered who she was really talking about — Bananas and Furball, or me and Summer? I mostly agreed that it'd be great if everyone got along, but it wasn't very practical. Or likely. Some pairings were like baking soda and vinegar — they exploded when combined. Forcing them together only made a mess.

I thought about that while I chewed and discreetly delivered a bit of my burrito to the under-table cleanup crew. What was it that made some friendships click and others fall apart?

It was quiet except for the sound of chewing when Dad suddenly perked up. "Do they know *what* killed Madame's cats?" he asked.

I shook my head. "They thought maybe it was poison, but they did a blood test and didn't find anything toxic. Just some elevated vitamin levels."

Dad squinted, thinking. "Some vitamins can be dangerous at high levels," he said, taking his final bite. "Like vitamin A. And C, come to think of it."

"Dangerous? I thought vitamins were good for you," Sam balked.

Dad finished chewing and washed it down with the last of his milk. "Vitamins can be very beneficial in the right doses, but too much of anything can be harmful. Even too much burrito." He pushed back from the table and patted his belly to demonstrate how close he was to burrito overdose.

"But are too many vitamins dangerous, or *lethal*?" I asked. There was a big difference between sick and dead.

Dad cocked his head so he could see under the table. I could feel Dodge licking his chops after his burrito dessert, but if Dad knew, he didn't say anything. He just looked thoughtful. "Both."

Both. The word stuck in my brain and the list of household poisons from the other day popped into my head to join it. *Too much of anything . . . More than one way to kill a cat . . .* Maybe Erica Bloom's fertilizer alone hadn't been enough to do the job.

"I think I'll head into the office to do a little research," Dad said as he got up from the table. Sam started to clear and I climbed the stairs to my room with Dodge, Bananas, and my iPod.

The dynamic duo curled up on my bed while I opened the laptop and popped in my headphones. I plunked down next to them, glad it was finally time to investigate.

I let the audio files play in the background as I surfed the local news sites online. I read the headlines, the obituaries, the police blotter. Nothing. Then I searched "Henry Kales." Nothing. Next I moved on to "fertilizer." Not much. Just the minor warnings I'd already seen.

After that I tried "vitamins," typing in the word "overdose" along with it. Dad was right! Excessive vitamins were totally toxic, and every year several people died from hypervitaminosis. It wasn't hard to picture humans overdoing it on vitamins — people almost always thought more equaled better. But a cat had to be forced to swallow a pill. I'd administered meds to more than one kitty at Pet Rescue, and it was hard *and* dangerous — even when the tablet was covered in butter. The thought of somebody trying to make Madame's cats overdose on vitamins seemed ridiculous. They'd be slashed from wrist to elbow!

There had to be something else to it, some piece I was missing. While my mind leapt from thought to thought in search of a connection, I scanned articles online and half listened to the recorded calls on my headphones.

It was easy to give part of my brain over to listening to other people's emergencies. It was like having the radio on, only instead of oldies or hot hits, I'd tuned in to the "I locked my toddler in the car" and "There's an alarm going off on Beattie Street" station.

The calls were sort of interesting, but I was really waiting for a specific one, or two. After a while I started to get sleepy. I put down the computer and lay back on my pillows, still listening. Dodge climbed off of my bed and onto his — ready to hunker down — and Bananas was right with him. My hand dropped over the edge of my mattress, onto Dodge's fur. I rolled over. I closed my eyes, just for a second. I could finish this tomorrow, I told myself. I could set my alarm and wake up early. I felt myself drifting into sleep.

"That old witch will be sorry if she doesn't keep those cats out of my yard!" a familiar voice suddenly screeched. My eyes flew open and I sat up fast. I'd been waiting to hear Madame LeFarge, but this was Erica Bloom!

"If the authorities don't take care of this problem, I will!" The fury in Erica's voice made my heart race. She was serious — dead serious. I made a mental note to ask Mom if Erica was a frequent caller. I'd heard about the one incident with the cat poop, but that had been a while back. These files were recent.

Then the next message came on. This time it *was* the voice I'd been waiting to hear — Madame LeFarge — and she was in a panic. "Someone is in my house!" she whispered, hoarse and frantic. Chills went up my spine — I could feel her fear. "There's a person in my house!" she repeated desperately. Then the line clicked on the recording; that was it.

I skipped back to listen to the time stamps on the call, and my already-racing heart thumped faster as I confirmed what I'd suspected. The call had been made last Friday night.

The night Madame LeFarge died.

CHAPTER 27

I tried to wait for Cassie to get home. I really did. Even Bananas tried. But we were tired. Tired of sitting at home. Tired of The Cat. Tired of lying around. We needed to get out. Get some air. Get to sniffing.

I never thought I'd say this about a cat, but The Kid was a good sniffer. She'd already sniffed out a meaty treat that'd been behind the stove for ages. Then she slipped back there to nab it. And she shared. We licked our chops and knew we'd done all we could in the house. School wasn't out yet, but we needed to be.

I hit the back-door latch and let The Kid go first. I didn't think about the fence until we were both in the backyard. *Aw, woof.* I could clear the fence, no problem. I'd done it tons of times. But not with a cat on my back.

I started to pace. I started to pant. The Kid kept cool as a collie. She had a plan. She prowled. She disappeared in the long grass along the inside of the fence — the part The Brother never mowed. She found a gap big enough to squeeze through. The Kid was out before I was!

A running leap and I was at her side. I crouched low so she could climb onto my back, and we were off.

I knew where I wanted to go. Back to Prospect Street — the scene of the crime. I wanted to scope things out. Dig up clues. Crack this case open. Cassie'd been searching for clues last night, with the buzzers in her ears and computer on her lap. We were making progress. Or she was. I wanted to pull my weight, too. But I didn't do tech. I did down-and-dirty investigating. It was time for down and dirty.

I tried to look casual, trotting up the sidewalk with a cat on my back. But it was hard to be low profile when you were toting a kitten. Luckily nobody seemed to be around. Doors were closed. Curtains were drawn. I didn't even see any cars in driveways. I slowed before we got to the watcher's house. Even if everyone else was at work, Kales would probably be out. Watching. He was always on his porch. Except today. Today Kales's porch was empty. Maybe it had finally gotten too cold.

The Kid jumped off her perch when we got close to her old house. She let out a sad "meowf." I knew what she meant. It hurt to go back to the places your people used to be. I left her to prowl and headed toward the houses on the other side of Madame's. I was a Labrador's length from Heinz's hedges when I got that same smell in my snout. Fish. Oily fish.

I sniffed long and deep. The smell wasn't coming from the dirt or the bushes. It was sort of . . . everywhere. It reminded me of that day on Heinz's porch. With the flyers. He'd smelled like fish. And horseradish. He'd been smiley. Cassie thought he was nice. But there was something about the guy I didn't like. He was too friendly. Twitchy eyed. Slippery. Yeah. Slippery. Like a fish.

I checked Heinz's porch. The side yards. Tried to get closer. No luck. No low windows. No way in.

I sniffed Bloom's yard next. It was fishy there, too. But different. The fishiness was mixed with other smells. Blood. Bone. Wood. Gardener smells. Gardeners liked to dig. They liked stinky stuff. They liked to dig stinky stuff in around their plants. Like the stuff from the bag in Erica's trash. But that bag had been full. She wasn't digging it into the dirt. She was giving it to the garbage truck.

I sniffed around to the back of Bloom's. I found an old ladder leaning against the fence. Right between Heinz's yard and Bloom's garden. I wanted to see what was on the other side. My choices were limited — over or under. Before I could decide, The Kid was there, scaling the fence like it was nothing. *Woof.* Built-in equipment.

"Meowf!" Bananas called down. "Meowf! Meowf!" There was something on the other side she wanted me to see. Only I didn't have equipment for over. I had equipment for under. And under wouldn't be discreet. Under would leave evidence of our investigation.

I'd have to go over, too. I eyed the ladder. Most dogs don't do ladders. But I wasn't most dogs. I'd learned how to climb at the academy. I was trained. It wasn't easy, but I could do it.

I moved slowly, paw over paw. I shifted my weight and placed my feet on the narrow rungs. Paw over paw over paw. I ignored the gaps. Then I was up. I could see.

I peered into Heinz's yard. It was full of stuff. Long, weedy grass. Rotting leaves. Moldy furniture. Trash. Lots of trash, like big cardboard boxes and Styrofoam packing.

I looked at The Kid. Was this what she wanted to show me? She caught my eye, then turned back to the house.

Finally I saw what she saw. An open window. A slightly open window.

I let out a low "growf." I couldn't help it. I wanted to get into that house. I had a feeling in my whiskers. There was something in there I should see. Maybe that was what The Kid was thinking, too. She could probably fit through the window crack no problem. But she was just a kid. It wouldn't be fair to send her in, especially alone.

There was nothing else I could do here. Not without Cassie. I was about to climb down when The Kid leaped into the yard. She crouched low and prowled toward the window. What was she doing?

I wanted to bark, to tell her to come back. But barking could've gotten us in trouble.

I watched her creep through the grass. Barely disturbing a blade. She was good. Really good. Part of me wanted her to keep going. To get in. Another part didn't. It was too dangerous. But it didn't matter what my parts wanted. The Kid had her own ideas.

She made it to the window and climbed right through. The tip of her tail disappeared and my tongue came out of my mouth. Nervous. I panted. Watched. Worried. My legs got shaky.

It wasn't easy for a dog to stay on a ladder. Even a trained dog. Even a top dog. I stayed, though. I waited. And watched. And worried.

I heard a car roll into the driveway. Heinz's car. *Aw, woof.* I couldn't stay anymore. Staying would jeopardize everything. I scrambled down and got out of sight. I ended up in Banana's shrub — the one she'd shared with Madame LeFarge. It smelled like falling leaves, Bananas, and Madame. The living Madame.

I held perfectly still. Heinz got out of his car. My good ear twitched. He was whistling. Happy. Too happy? I hoped The Kid would come streaking out when he cracked the front door. She didn't. The door opened. The door closed. Now Bill and Bananas were both inside! And I only trusted one of them.

I lay down. I panted. I had to decide. Should I stay or should I go?

My instincts said go — don't get caught. My training said stay.

I was well trained.

I stayed.

CHAPTER 28

Bounding down the school steps, I glanced at my phone: 3:13. I wouldn't be home for at least two more hours — maybe three. And I'd already been gone for almost seven! "Sorry, Dodge," I murmured under my breath. I really *was* sorry, too. I felt bad for leaving Dodge and Bananas cooped up all day. But I had some super important stuff to do, and I was barely going to make it home for dinner — even with Hayley and Alicia's help.

"Okay, Cass, what's our first stop?" Hayley asked as she unlocked her bike beside me.

"Pet Rescue."

Alicia and Hayley nodded in unison, looking super serious. They'd really gone out of their way to help me, and were stepping up yet again. "Right after we grab some smoothies at Hava Java," I added. "On me."

"Yesss!" Alicia pumped her fist like she'd scored a goal, and we rolled off toward sweet sustenance. Two Mango Tangos and a Berry Me Sweetheart later, we arrived at PR.

Hayley slurped the last bit of her smoothie as we pushed through the door. I looked around for the trash and felt a tug on my sleeve. "Isn't that . . ." Hayley trailed off and I followed her gaze. What I saw made me stop in my tracks: Erica Bloom!

The toxic gardener was talking to Gwen. I was aware, of course, that everyone was innocent until proven guilty. In my mind, however, I'd already decided that Erica was up to no good. She could try to hide it, but I'd heard the anger in her voice, seen the poison in her trash. She was a kitty killer, and who knew what else.

"Thanks so much," Erica said, smiling at Gwen. "I'll be back for another visit tomorrow." I felt my forehead wrinkle and quickly hid behind Hayley as Erica left the shelter.

Inside, I was seething. Who, exactly, was she visiting? Was she here at PR to try to finish off the other cats? "What was that about?" I demanded as soon as Erica was gone.

"Cassie!" Gwen beamed at me from behind the reception desk, not noticing that I was upset. Then she yowled. "Ow!"

Something was struggling in her arms. Something orange and white and sharp. Bananas! Wait, what? "What's she doing here?" I sputtered.

The anger I'd been directing at Erica suddenly shifted. "Sam!" I spat my sister's name like a curse. Sam was the only person in our house who'd bring Bananas back to PR. Apparently she'd only *acted* like she cared last night at dinner. She was obviously as anxious to get rid of the kitten as ever, and had brought Bananas in to spite me!

"Whoa!" Gwen held up her scratched hand. "Take it easy, Cass. Sam didn't bring Bananas in, that woman did."

"Erica Bloom?" I felt like I was losing my mind.

"Yeah. She lives next to the LeFarge place and found Bananas in her backyard. She coaxed her into a crate with some tuna and brought her here to be with the rest of the cats."

I stared at Bananas, wishing she could tell me what the heck had happened. But the only one talking was Gwen.

"Oh, and guess what? Your flyers are working! We're getting adoption interest in Madame's cats. Someone came in this morning and wants two, and Ms. Bloom is interested in three!"

Hearing that, Bananas reached out a paw and scratched Gwen again. "Ow!" Gwen yelped. "How have you been living with this monster? Finding a home for you is not going to be easy," she scolded, looking into the kitten's green eyes.

Bananas let out a plaintive mew, as if she understood.

"You're right about that," I agreed. My anger was fading, but my suspicions about Erica weren't.

Gwen set Bananas on the ground. "Go ahead. Be free. I'm ready for a break from those talons!"

Bananas mewed again and I swear the little cat gave her a smug look. Alicia cracked up. I might have laughed, too, but my mind was looping on something Gwen had said: *Ms. Bloom is interested in three!*

"You know Erica is the woman who threatened Madame LeFarge *and* her cats, right?" I blurted. "I think she was trying to poison them. Dodge and I found evidence in her trash. She's a total suspect in the Salt and Pepper murder!"

Gwen, Hayley, and Alicia all looked stunned.

"She *hated* Madame's cats!" I insisted.

"Her? Really?" Gwen was incredulous. "But Ginger

responded better to her than she does to me, and she bonded with Cinnamon and Trouble, too."

"Trouble?" Alicia asked, smiling. "Is that a name?"

"Yeah," Gwen confirmed. "I was calling him Chili, but he's always riling up the other cats, so I changed it."

I smiled at that. Gwen was great at naming animals. But my smile faded quickly, because the other thing Gwen was great at was reading people. She had a sixth sense about prospective pet owners and could tell who'd treat a pet like family and who'd get sick of caring for an animal once the cute factor wore off. She thought Erica was a candidate — a thought that didn't mesh with anything I knew about her.

It was possible Erica was trying to throw off suspicion by coming in and appearing concerned — like she did when she told me she missed Madame. But if that was it, she deserved an Academy Award for best actress.

"Hey, don't we have work to do?" Hayley asked, poking me in the ribs and pulling me out of my thoughts. My friends were standing by, waiting for instructions.

"Oh, right. Sorry. Hayley and Alicia are helping out again today, okay?"

"We'll take all the assistance we can get!" Gwen said, getting on the intercom to call Taylor, another PR regular, to the front desk. A minute later Taylor loped in with two dogs on leashes. He flipped his dark curls and gave Alicia and Hayley a lazy smile.

"I can help walk," Hayley quickly volunteered. Alicia and I rolled our eyes as she headed out the door with the Quest High sophomore. Puppy love.

Four hands were definitely better than two when it came to cleaning cat cages. Alicia and I worked well together, and quickly. Alicia didn't complain, either. Okay, once I caught her pulling a face and wrinkling her nose while we were changing some especially stinky litter. But who could blame her?

"I never said working at Pet Rescue was glamorous!" I joked.

"I'll take cuteness over glamour any day." Alicia giggled, watching Ginger tenderly groom Parsley's ear, and then playfully bite it.

With the extra help I was finished at PR way faster than I would've been alone. Maybe too fast for Hayley. Alicia and I shared another eye roll as Hayley lingered over her good-bye with Taylor, and this time Hayley spotted our goofy expressions.

"What?" she asked, all innocence. Which totally cracked us up, even Hayley. My best friend may have had a crush on Taylor, but, thank goodness, she was still her goofy self. I was smiling to myself when I remembered my next stop: the hospital to see Duke.

"Do you want us to come with you?" Hayley asked. My grave expression had brought her down off her cloud, too.

I shook my head. "No, I'm good. I'm going to have to fudge the truth to get in to see Duke without an adult. It'll be easier if I'm alone."

Alicia nodded, and Hayley gave me a good-luck hug. "Text us later, ok?"

"I'll be holding my breath," Alicia added.

I grinned slyly. "Well, at least you got plenty of practice while we cleaned the litter boxes." I pinched my nose to illustrate.

Alicia groaned. "Don't remind me!"

I slung my backpack over my shoulders and we rode together for a little while, then split up when I turned toward Bellport General Hospital.

It felt strange to ride alone. No friends. No Dodge. But after a few more turns I was rolling into the hospital parking lot. *Relax*, I told myself. *Duke's going to be fine. You got this*. And I knew I did, but I couldn't help thinking that I would feel a lot better if Dodge were with me.

CHAPTER 29

I sat under the bush for a long time. Waiting. Listening. Hoping. Okay, so maybe I fell asleep. For a second or two. Stakeouts have never been my thing — I'm a dog of action.

When I woke up the light had changed. I couldn't be sure if Bananas was still in Heinz's house. What if she'd slipped out? What if she'd been caught?

I hoped The Kid was okay. I hoped. I hoped. I hoped.

I crawled out from under the bush to try to pick up a trail. My friend The Nose could have sniffed out The Kid in no time. The Nose was a basset — best sniffers in the business. Only he was getting up there in age.

Spent a lot of time curled up in his window seat. Snoring. And anyway, he wasn't here. I just had me. Me, my shepherd nose, and more cat trails than a porcupine had quills.

I put my nose down. I sniffed. Here. There. I picked up one trail. Then another. And another. From Bloom's to LeFarge's to Heinz's and back. The scent tracks crisscrossed all over the neighborhood. Too many of them. *Woof.* I was sniffing in circles.

Too bad The Nose lived most of the way back home. . . . Home!

Home gave me an idea. Maybe The Kid managed to slip out of Heinz's but didn't know I was waiting for her. Maybe she went where she thought she'd find me. Maybe she went home!

I put my nose to the ground and smelled my way toward Salisbury Drive. I was happy to be moving, but my tail was low. I felt bad for putting The Kid in a dangerous situation. She'd jumped into the yard herself. She'd gone into the house alone. But I should have stopped her! I should have been her backup!

I whined. I wished I'd stopped her. But I wasn't even sure that I could have. The Kid had a mind of her own.

And she was all claws when she was mad. My nose was proof of that!

I bit back a whine and started to run. *Please*, I thought as I hurled myself toward home. *Please, please, please let her be okay.*

CHAPTER 30

Bellport General was an old brick building with a new glass-and-steel wing on one side. I rode up the path toward the facility feeling like I'd swallowed a frozen rock. I looked around for a bike rack by the entrance, to no avail. The realization that most people didn't arrive at the hospital by bicycle made the cold rock in my gut expand. I locked my bike to a tree and forced myself to walk through the door.

Inside the lobby, I was not-so-warmly welcomed by a woman at the information desk. Her stern, steady gaze didn't shrink my tummy boulder a single bit.

I gulped. "Hi. I'm here to see my uncle Duke. Duke MacLean."

She continued to stare. Silently.

"It's still visiting hours, right?" I squeaked.

"Is there an adult with you?" she finally asked, looking past me.

I nodded, maybe too much. "Yeah, my dad's parking the car. He'll be right in, but visiting hours end soon, and Uncle Duke is super lonely up there. . . ." I hoped Duke's room wasn't on the ground floor. I wanted to sound like I knew my way around — like I'd been to see him before.

Desk Lady narrowed her eyes at me, hesitating. Then she finally started to nod, slowly. I was free to go. I took two steps toward the elevator bank and turned.

"Oh, uh, what's Uncle Duke's room number again? Duke MacLean?" I reminded her.

She checked her computer screen. "Three sixteen."

"Right, of course. Three sixteen." I touched my palm to my forehead and forced myself to walk slowly to the elevators, waiting for what seemed like forever until the doors opened. As the elevator lifted I finally allowed myself to take a breath. *Whew.* I'd gotten past the first hurdle. Also, Duke couldn't be *too* bad off if I was allowed to visit.

The doors opened onto the third floor nurses' station. Not wanting to draw attention to myself, I turned quickly and walked to the left, like I knew where I was going. My Converse squeaked on the tile and the sound sent a shiver up my spine. Or maybe the shiver was from being in the hospital. Hospitals creeped me out almost as much as Dad's office. For about the billionth time I wished Dodge was there to lay a warm, wet kiss on my hand and let me know everything was all right.

I had just turned the corner when I spotted Bill Heinz walking toward me. I wondered what he was doing there and briefly considered saying hello, then thought better of it. I bent down to tie my shoe instead, letting my hair make a curtain around my face. I probably didn't need to hide, because Bill didn't even notice me. He was totally preoccupied, muttering to himself and moving fast. I tilted my head to try to catch what he was saying but only got a few stray words: "broken agreements" and "contract." The dude was hopping mad — not the friendly fish-fry guy he'd been at his house — and I was glad I'd gotten out of his way.

I was almost back to the elevators when I found room 316. The door was open and after knocking lightly I stepped inside. "Hello?"

"Cassandra!" Duke was sitting up in bed. He looked pale and tired, but smiled broadly when he saw me.

Whatever was ailing him hadn't diminished his spirit. "So nice of you to come!"

"Wild horses couldn't keep me away," I said, using a phrase Dad liked. "And neither could the cranky lady at the reception desk," I added, putting my hand up to my mouth like it was a big secret. "I had to come see how you're doing."

Duke grinned. "Well, the old ticker's still going," he said, patting his chest. "And the doc says my liver will recover." Then he paused and gazed up at the ceiling before adding somberly, "Unlike our little business."

"Your business is sick, too?" I wasn't totally surprised to hear that Duke's "little miracles" weren't going to make them millions, but I was curious to find out why. "What happened?"

"Turns out it was the Pepper-Uppers that put me in here," he said, raising his eyebrows high on his wrinkly forehead. "Yup. Too much of a good thing. Too much vitamin A — that's what taxed my liver, and my stressed liver put my heart in a state."

I couldn't believe what I was hearing. It was so familiar! "Yeah, too much vitamin A can cause all sorts of problems," I said, nodding dumbly.

"Yup. Especially for an old guy." Duke twiddled his

thumbs. "I guess that young fella thought he was onto something with his *mega* omega-3s, but it wasn't anything good. There's a reason you need FDA approval before marketing, you know." Duke shook his head, his twinkly eyes narrowed. I wasn't sure what to say.

"I guess we jumped the gun a little, trying something untested. And we probably seemed like an easy target — a bunch of oldsters anxious to feel young and increase their retirement to boot. Old fools." Duke seemed a little embarrassed.

"You're no fools," I told him, and meant it. The folks at Home Away had given me advice about all kinds of things. They were smart *and* wise!

"Maybe we just got carried away," Duke said, smiling again. "But if that slippery salesman thinks we're too feeble to pull out of his snake-oil business, he's dead wrong. We may lose everything, but we're going to make darn sure Mr. Heinz does, too."

"Heinz? Like Bill Heinz?" I asked, unable to believe my ears. "He's the guy behind Pepper-Uppers?"

"That's the one." Duke nodded. "Sold us a bunch of garbage." With a shaking hand he took a pill bottle out of the bag by his bed and pitched it into the trash can by the door. It landed with a clunk. "Haven't lost my touch!" he chortled.

Bill Heinz, my mind repeated. I wanted to grab the bottle right back out of the trash. The pieces of the puzzle were falling together, but the image kept changing. I thought I'd been putting together a picture of a sea otter, only it suddenly looked more like a rhinoceros!

"Mwuf." A strange sound interrupted my thoughts, muffled but familiar. "Meowf!"

Duke blinked at me. "What was that?"

I smirked, suddenly knowing exactly what it was and why my backpack felt so heavy. Bananas! The sneaky cat stuck her head out of my pack. "Now, how did you manage that?" I asked her. The last time I'd seen Bananas she was at Pet Rescue . . . in the lobby . . . next to my backpack! She must have crawled in because it smelled like our favorite dog.

"Meowf!" she repeated, satisfied.

Duke's face lit up and he reached out a hand to pet her.

"Careful," I warned. "Her cuteness is deceptive." But Bananas let him lift her out of the pack and settle her on the bed. In fact, she walked right onto his lap and rubbed the top of her head all over his grizzled chin, purring!

I stared, speechless.

"Just who is this little angel?" Duke asked, loving the affection.

Angel? I thought. But watching the two of them, I knew for certain that Bananas wasn't a devil. She was just very, very particular. She loved Dodge. And now she loved Duke. "Duke MacLean," I said, "meet Bananas."

"Why, hello, Bananas." Duke stroked her back.

"Meowf!" Bananas returned his greeting.

I was smiling at the amazing development in room 316 when there was a light rap on the door. "How are we doing in here?" a nurse called.

My eyes widened. I wasn't supposed to be here, and neither was Bananas! Duke didn't miss a beat, though. He quickly shoved the kitten under his covers.

"Just fine," he called to the nurse, giving me a wink.

The nurse nodded approvingly as she came into the room. She glanced at a chart on the wall and took Duke's blood pressure. Duke shifted a little, lifting his knees to give Bananas more room. I could still hear Bananas purring, so I coughed and started to riffle through my backpack to cover the noise. It worked . . . except the covers started to move!

"Meowf!" Bananas wanted out!

"What was that?" the nurse asked, looking up from her watch. "Bless you!" Duke said loudly.

I quickly put a hand in front of my face like I'd just sneezed. The nurse stared. "You sneeze just like a cat," she said, smiling at me while she removed the blood pressure thingy. "I'll be back with your meds in a minute," she told Duke.

"And you two better get going," Duke said in a whisper, his eyes twinkling. He lifted Bananas out of the bedclothes and gave her a kiss on the nose.

"Time to be quiet," I told the kitten as I pushed her back into my pack.

"Mrroow!" she objected.

"You chose this, you little stowaway," I reminded her. I zipped the kitten in and squeezed Duke's arm. "I'm so glad you're okay. I'll come back if I can," I promised.

"That would be lovely, Cassandra," Duke replied. "And, please, bring our friend."

The nurse was coming back in as we headed out. I glanced down, not wanting to look her in the eyes, and found myself staring into the trash. The label on Duke's bottle of Pepper-Uppers stared right back. "Shark liver oil — the richest source of vitamins and omega-3s." The blurb was framed in a bright red burst. I quickly reached into the can and grabbed the bottle. Then the stowaway and I headed for the exit, for home, and for Dodge.

CHAPTER 31

I ran. And ran. And ran. All the way home. Okay, most of the way home. I was near our corner when I spotted Summer ahead of me. On her bike. I slowed to a walk and lifted my nose, to see if I could smell a little something good in her bike basket. *Sniff, sniff, sniff.*

Nothing.

Summer's basket was empty. Muffet wasn't inside, which was too bad. I liked Muffet — liked her a lot. She was full of good surprises. I really could've used a good surprise.

I picked up the pace again as I turned onto Salisbury Drive. I kept on running. And hoping. I circled around the back of the Sullivans'. I leaped the fence, going in the way we'd come out. I barked anxiously at the kitchen door. I panted. I needed to get in. To find Bananas.

Finally The Brother opened the door. I was panting so hard I couldn't give him a thank-you lick. I stopped by my bowls and took a long drink. Then a long sniff. Water dripped off my tongue while I logged the air. Cassie wasn't home. I knew that. And Bananas wasn't, either.

My tail drooped. My hope drooped. If Bananas wasn't home, she was still in Heinz's house. And if she was still in Heinz's house, she had to be stuck. Or trapped. Or hurt. Or . . . *Woof.*

I needed to get into Heinz's. *Click, click, click, click.* I paced. *Click, click, click, click.* Back and forth. *Click, click, click, click.* In front of the door. *Click, click, click, click.* My tail hung low. My ears hung low. I was responsible. Full of guilt. A bad dog. But I wasn't a bad dog. I was a good dog. A great dog. A trained dog.

I could make this right. I could make a plan.

"Woof!" I barked at the back door. "Woof! Woof!" I barked again and again. I couldn't open it myself. Not when humans were home. And I needed out. Out. Out. Out!

Finally The Brother heard me through his ear buzzers and came up from his den. "Didn't I just let you in?" he asked. "You okay, buddy?" His face was worried and his eyes scanned the kitchen floor. He thought I was acting weird because I'd made a mess. And I had. But it wasn't a "pile on the floor" kind of mess. The mess I'd made would be harder to clean up.

"Woof!" I barked again.

"Okay, okay." The Brother let me out.

I waited until I heard the latch click shut. Then I leaped the fence and started to run. I'd gotten Bananas into this and I would get her out. I just needed a little help. . . .

CHAPTER 32

"Hold still," I told Bananas. I was pedaling home as fast as I could with an orange kitten scrambling around in my backpack. Her claws pierced the nylon fabric and went right through my jacket more sharply than the cold wind as she pulled herself up and poked her head out for a better view.

"I don't know how Dodge does it," I murmured, wincing.

"Meowf," Bananas replied in my ear. She probably knew where we were headed and was anxious to get there, too.

I stood on my pedals, exhaling steam and pumping hard up the last incline. I let out a groan — not at the effort, at the view. Up ahead, sprawled on the pavement next to her bike, was Summer Hill.

"Oh, darn," I muttered as we approached. Her chain was off and the tires were spinning slowly. I wanted to pretend I hadn't seen her and ride on by. Bananas must have picked up on my thoughts, because she ducked back inside my pack. "Is there enough room in there for both of us?" I asked. I longed to hide, too, but instead found myself putting on the brakes.

"Are you okay?" I asked, coasting to a stop.

Summer looked up at me, her face half covered with her blonde hair. I couldn't tell if the twisted expression behind it was pain, surprise, or an attempt to fight back tears.

She cleared her throat. "Um, no," she said.

I silently parked my bike and righted hers, leaving her to check her knees and elbows for scrapes. Summer wasn't good at mechanical stuff. When we were friends, I was the one who pumped tires and put chains back on.

I flipped her bike upside down, balancing it on the handlebars. Lining the chain up on the big gear in front, I spun the pedals forward. With a *clickety-clunk*, the chain slid back on.

We didn't talk. I could feel Summer watching, though, and when I glanced her way she gave me a very un-Summer-like look. She looked . . . softer. Maybe even bruised. I wondered if she was still trying not to cry when she opened her mouth.

I braced for tears or a nasty comment — I wasn't sure which.

"I'm sorry about stepping on the scrapbook," she said quietly.

"Huh?" I said stupidly. An apology was *not* what I was expecting!

"I guess I was hurt. I sort of wished you'd sent it to me. I think . . . sometimes . . . well, sometimes I just wish . . ." She drifted off, and I found myself wondering what she was wishing. It seemed impossible for Summer to be sorry. For anything. Maybe she had a minor head injury.

I was trying to think of what to say when Bananas stuck her head out of my backpack and spoke for me. "Meowf!"

Summer blinked rapidly and stared at my shoulder. "Is that a cat?"

"That's Bananas," I replied.

"No, seriously. There's a cat in your bag." She pointed like she'd spotted a miniature Sasquatch.

"I know." I couldn't help smiling as I explained. "Her *name* is Bananas. She's one of Madame LeFarge's."

I cranked the pedals one last time, making sure the chain was going to stay, and turned the bike right side up.

Summer stood, brushed herself off, and took the handlebars. Then she reached over to pet Bananas before I could warn her. Lo and behold, Bananas accepted the pet! *Wonders never cease*, I thought. I wasn't just marveling at Bananas, either. I was kind of stunned by myself, because — amazingly — I didn't *want* Bananas to scratch her. In fact, for the first time in practically forever, I was standing next to Summer without feeling a strong urge to trip her or spill something on her.

"She's pretty cute," Summer said, tickling Bananas behind the ears.

"You should see her with Dodge. She thinks she's a dog," I said before I could stop myself. Why did I tell Summer that?

Summer laughed. "Really? That's so funny! Remember those YouTube videos we used to watch of odd animal pairs — the tortoise and the baby hippo, and the dog and tiger cub?"

I blinked. I totally remembered. But somehow I'd managed to forget that I remembered.

"What happened to the rest of Madame's cats?"

Summer asked without pausing. It was like she cared or something, and it was freaking me out!

"They're at Pet Rescue waiting to be adopted," I mumbled. I looked at her pupils to see if they were dilated — she could've gotten a concussion when she fell off her bike. But her eyes seemed normal as she nodded thoughtfully.

"My aunt Marissa was thinking about getting a cat," she said. "You want me to talk to her?"

"Actually, that would be great," I said. I was starting to feel like I was having an out-of-body experience. This was getting weirder by the second!

Summer nodded, climbing onto her bike. "Okay, I will. And thanks." She patted her handlebars.

"Sure," I mumbled as she pedaled away.

Bananas meowfed in my ear.

"Yup, I totally agree." I was glad the cat had been with me to witness the weirdness. "Either we just made a stop on an alien planet or we've had a close encounter with Summer Hill's not-so-evil twin!"

CHAPTER 33

All it took was one bark. One bark outside the sparkly doggy door and Muffet was heading right toward me. The Maltese whimpered. She wagged. She sniffed. She was happy to see me. I wagged back. I was happy to see her, too. The little dog was going to be a big help. I just hoped she wasn't a major cat chaser. At least not today.

Our noses touched and Muffet understood I was on a case. She was in. We took off toward Prospect Street in a hurry.

When we got to Heinz's, though, I realized we had a problem. A tall problem. The fence.

Muffet wasn't ladder trained like I was. And even if she were, the rungs were too far apart for her legs. She couldn't go over; she'd have to go under!

We sniffed out a soft, hidden spot in Bloom's yard, at the back of a flower bed. We started to dig. Paw. Scrape. Paw. Scrape. It felt good to be doing something. Unearthing smells. Making dirt fly. We dug as fast as we could. The hole didn't have to be big. Just Muffet-size.

When we could see light from the other side, Muffet wriggled through. She got covered in dirt. *Woof!* She looked like the burglar she was about to become. And way better than she did in Summer's froufy outfits.

I climbed the ladder to see into Heinz's yard and bark directions if I needed to. I didn't need to. Muffet saw the basement window and slid right through. Good Muffet.

I climbed another rung. And another. I was at the very top when I heard a noise. Someone was coming — again. I froze. I looked around for a place to hide. Then the best smells in the world hit my nostrils. Grass. Soap. A hint of bacon. Cassie! Cassie was my favorite. My absolute favorite.

My tail wagged. Fast and hard. But wagging on a ladder was not a good idea. I had to jump before I fell. So I jumped. And I landed in Heinz's yard. *Woof.*

A moment later I saw Cassie's head, peering over the fence. "Dodge?" she shouted in a whisper. "Dodge! I just went home to look for you. What's going on? How'd you know about Bill?"

Bill? I wasn't here for Bill Heinz. I was here for The Kid. I gave Cassie my "heel" look. I didn't want to bark, but I needed her by my side. I needed her to follow. I made sure she saw and headed for the house.

Then I heard it. Coming from Cassie's bag.

"Meowf."

There was only one cat that mewed like that. The Kid! Cassie'd found The Kid!

Cassie jumped down into Heinz's yard and crouched in the grass. The Kid climbed out of her pack and scampered over. She rubbed on my legs with her motor going. Loud. If I had a motor, I'd have been revved up, too. Yeah. I was glad to see her safe. Really glad.

I gave her a good sniff, to see where she'd been. The Kid smelled like dust and thyme. She also smelled like Cassie's homework, Pet Rescue, and Erica Bloom!

That explained a lot. Bloom must have nabbed The Kid when she came out of Heinz's house. While I was under the bush. Bloom probably took her to Pet Rescue. Yeah. That made sense. Cassie would find her there. She probably stashed The Kid in her pack. But how'd Cassie know where to find me?

"Woof!" I barked. I couldn't help it. I was so relieved. But Cassie shushed me.

"Quiet, Dodge," she whispered. Her head was cocked toward Heinz's house. Then I heard another bark. Muffet's!

Cassie heard it, too.

Woof. I was so busy wagging over one friend being *out* of trouble I forgot I'd gotten another friend *in* trouble.

Cassie gazed at me. Serious. "That's Muffet in there, isn't it?"

I stared back a "yes."

"So what's the plan?" She scanned the messy yard and noticed the window. I led her to the door and paused. The plan was that Muffet would rescue The Kid. Only the plan had changed. Now we needed to rescue Muffet.

Get her out, I whined.

Cassie tried the door. Locked. The window wouldn't work for either of us. Too small. But The Kid could fit. And she did. She slipped inside while I started sniffing. The scent of snails and metal wafted up from a pot of dead flowers. I pawed at the base. Cassie tipped the pot on its side and . . . bingo! We'd found the spare key. We were in!

CHAPTER 34

I slid the key into the lock and turned the handle. *Is it breaking and entering if you don't actually take anything?* I wondered. I was pretty sure it was. I was also pretty sure that was why my heart felt like it was trying to leap out of my chest. Taking a breath, I stepped through Bill Heinz's back door with Dodge beside me.

The smell inside was overwhelming. The whole place reeked of fish. Like more fish than anyone should ever eat or . . . I grasped the bottle in my pocket, the one I'd taken out of Duke's trash. We *were* talking about more than anyone should ever eat!

Knowing we were on the right trail helped calm my nerves a little. Dodge seemed to know we were close to breaking the case wide open, too. That must have been why he'd come here. Though I still wasn't clear on why he'd brought Muffet.

We followed Bananas to a small door in the kitchen. The door opened onto stairs leading to the basement. And if I thought the fish smell couldn't get any stronger? Well, I was wrong. I had to breathe through my mouth to keep from gagging, and even then I felt like I could taste it in the back of my throat. The smell was that thick.

Bananas zipped down the stairs like she'd done it a million times before, disappearing into the dark. She had the cat-eye advantage. Her paws were silent on the steps, but from the base of the stairs, in the blackness, I heard a familiar yip. Dodge plunged ahead of me, and I flipped on the lights and followed.

The basement room was dank and windowless. Lights hung from a low ceiling and the stainless steel tables that lined the walls were covered in equipment I didn't recognize. The shelves above were crowded with strange ingredients, bottles, and labels — it was a Pepper-Upper factory.

I felt dizzy. From the smell, yes. And also from the fact that I was surrounded by evidence — evidence that made everything click together.

"Woof!" Dodge called my attention to Bananas and a very dirty Muffet. They huddled together over a dark spot on the floor. Muffet had her nose pressed close while Bananas licked the oily stain.

"What is that?" I bent down to touch it and rubbed my fingers together. It was greasy. I gave a sniff and nearly barfed. "Ugh!" I spluttered. I'd found the source of the fish stink: fish oil! And I was betting this wasn't just any fish oil, but the source of the mega omega-3s. This was shark liver oil!

"Don't eat that," I told Bananas, waving her away from the spill. "You either," I told Muffet.

I examined the room, stunned. I'd set out to find my dog and wound up finding Bill Heinz's poison factory. Bill might have seemed like the friendly fish-fry guy, but he was as greedy as they got. The memory of his angry expression in the hospital, when he'd just learned that Duke wasn't going to sell the supplements that had almost killed him, made me make a few angry faces of my own. Bill was a crook! A scammer! A criminal! He'd been taking advantage of the nice people at Home Away to sell his untested, unsafe pills.

I pulled the bottle out of my pocket and peered at the label. In addition to omega-3s, the pills were loaded with vitamin A. And if Bananas knew just where to find a fishy treat, the rest of Madame's cats probably did, too. Licking up the overconcentrated fish oil spills and chowing down a bottle of Pepper-Uppers was almost certainly what had killed poor Salt and Pepper.

"Dodge, Heinz was the one poisoning cats, and the reason Duke is in the hospital," I announced. Dodge's ears went up. We'd found our perp, or at least his lab. "It's all here," I breathed. Except for the answer to the mystery we'd started out to solve: How did Madame LeFarge die?

I was about to start snapping pictures of the evidence with my phone when Muffet, Bananas, and Dodge all froze. I froze, too, straining to hear what they'd heard first. When I finally did, I sucked in my breath.

It was the rattle of keys in the front door.

CHAPTER 35

There wasn't enough room behind the warm tank for all of us. But we smushed together anyway.

Bananas sat on one side of me. Silent. Muffet sat on the other. Shivering. The Maltese wasn't nervous — she was excited. This was her second shakedown and the little pup was eating it up. Cassie hit the light and crouched with us.

We stayed as quiet as we could, which wasn't easy. Being in Heinz's house made my teeth itchy. The place reeked. Not in a bad way, but the smell was *really* strong. A growl tickled my throat.

Still. I kept still. I stayed. Hidden. Stealthy. Then the light blinked on and I felt exposed — like a poodle after a haircut. But Heinz couldn't see us. Not yet.

The fishy guy stomped down the stairs, talking to nobody. The metal smell of anger mixed with his pepper scent and the inescapable fish stink. It stung my nose.

"At least I've got their investment," he said, talking to himself. "They were the first ones dumb enough to sign the contract, but they won't be the last. I just need to find some other suckers to sell the stuff for me." He moved things around roughly, banging them together. I didn't know what he was talking about but I felt a change in Cassie's touch. She kept one hand on me and lifted Muffet up under her other arm. I think she knew how much my teeth itched. How much my teeth wanted to grab on to Heinz's pant leg and clamp down. Or maybe her teeth itched, too. Yeah. I wasn't the only one who wanted to take a bite out of Heinz.

"It's not *my* fault Duke MacLean had a weak heart," Heinz babbled. My ears twitched. He'd said Duke. Duke! That's what Cassie was talking about. Suddenly it all came together in my head: The fishy smell. The pills. The sick cats. Sick Duke. My teeth itched worse than ever.

There were a few of the nasty capsules on the floor behind the tank. With us. Bananas picked one up and I couldn't keep my growl in anymore. "Grrr!" *Drop it*, I growled. That stuff was dangerous. The Kid dropped the pill. She jumped onto my back and I stepped out from behind the tank.

Heinz stopped and turned. He took a step backward. He wasn't expecting us. I growled again. Low. Fierce. To let him know we meant business.

His face grew pale. His smell changed. Mixed with the cider vinegar scent of fear.

"We know you're guilty," Cassie said, stepping out behind me. She was talking about how he hurt Duke. About the bad pills.

"Meowf!" The Kid had something to say, too. Heinz was not going to get away with this.

The expression on Heinz's face said a lot. I'd seen that look before, on a chow who'd been caught eating a pair of leather boots. Shame. Guilt. He'd done Duke and the old-timers and the cats wrong. Big wrong.

Heinz raised his hands in the air. "I didn't mean to kill anyone!" he cried.

CHAPTER 36

I blinked in surprise, wondering if I'd heard right. *I didn't mean to kill anyone.* Kill anyone? *Kill* anyone? My jaw dropped. Bill didn't know about Salt and Pepper, and he definitely knew that Duke had survived the poisoning — he had to be talking about Madame LeFarge!

I steadied myself on a stainless steel table. I'd figured out that he was guilty of swindling the Home Awayers, and making the cats sick. But he'd just confessed to *killing* his *neighbor* — a much bigger crime.

My mind spinning, I blurted out the first question that came to me. "Were you already in the house when she called the police?"

Bill's face went even whiter — he didn't know I knew so much. "I was just trying to scare her a little — to tell her to mind her own business and keep her cats out of my basement!" he said in a rush. "She was a meddling busybody. If she'd have stopped poking around in my affairs, I —"

"Then you wouldn't have killed her?" I finished angrily.

"Look, all I wanted was to talk to her, maybe scare her a little. I needed *her* to see how it was to have uninvited guests for a change. Those cats of hers had been coming into my basement for weeks! And she was constantly spying on me. I didn't expect her to lose it like that. She was frantic, flailing her arms and screaming her head off."

Dodge took a step closer, growling. Bill backed against a wall of shelves.

"She was so riled up she tripped and hit her head on the kitchen counter. I didn't even push her! I didn't know she'd hit so hard, either. I thought she'd wake up and be a little freaked out. Maybe keep better control over her cats."

"You left her there unconscious?"

Bill swallowed. "I didn't think she'd *die*."

"You probably didn't think Duke would collapse from taking your poison pills, either. It sounds like you don't think about a lot of stuff."

"I never told that old man that he should take so many of my pills. Shark oil is potent stuff. It shouldn't be messed with."

"Neither should people's lives. You were taking advantage of the folks at Home Away and you knew it!"

Bill's eyes narrowed, and he raised his stubbly chin. "I just wanted to make a little money. Not my fault the old guy had to complicate things."

"Complicate things?" I balked. "By almost dying from taking *your* unregulated vitamins?"

Bill's face hardened into a steely mask, and I knew I'd pushed too far. His eyes darted around the room as he sized us up: A seventh grader, a pocket dog, and a German shepherd with a cat on his back — we looked more like a circus troop than the long arm of the law.

He stepped forward menacingly, and I suddenly wished I'd kept my big mouth shut. The tide was turning fast.

CHAPTER 37

My hackles rose and a growl rumbled in my throat. Heinz was more angry now. I could tell by the strong metallic smell coming off him, and the way he moved. He felt cornered. Nobody liked feeling cornered. No dog did, either. But Heinz was a bad man. Guilty.

"Rowf!" I lunged, knocking him off balance.

Muffet barked like a mad dog.

The Kid leaped to the ground and swiped at his ankle. "Reeeooooww!" Claws out.

That was all it took to bring the bad guy down. Down on his own fishy floor. I stood over his soft stomach. Bananas stood on his chest, and Muffet stood guard next to his head. We had him pinned. We held him there while Cassie pulled out her phone.

Then I heard them: voices. Right outside. And a familiar bark. Hero!

"In here!" Cassie called. Muffet yipped. The Kid and I held our ground — we had our man.

A minute later Officer Riley and Hero burst through the door and rushed down the stairs, followed by Summer. Summer? Yes, Summer. And she looked like she was back to her old self. Her eyes were narrow and angry.

"I told you somebody stole my dog!" she screeched, pointing at Cassie.

Aw, woof. This again?

"Are you holding Muffie hostage over that dumb book?" she huffed at Cassie. Her nose twitched and she eyed the floor with a shudder. "Eewwwww! What is this place? Some sort of torture chamber?"

Cassie stared at Summer like she had a second head, but didn't say a word. Officer Riley ignored her, too. Not even Hero paid any attention to Summer's whining. One look at me and The Kid, and Hero moved to flank us. Made extra sure Heinz stayed where he belonged. The whelp was learning.

"Officer Riley, I think you might want to take Mr. Heinz in for questioning," Cassie said. "He just confessed to killing Madame LeFarge."

Summer's mad eyes turned into surprised eyes.

"And thanks to Muffet's infiltration, I believe we can also prove that Mr. Heinz was running a fraudulent and dangerous business, swindling and poisoning two- and four-legged creatures with his illegal Pepper-Uppers." Cassie gave Muffet a pat on the head, still pretending Summer wasn't there. Riley busted out his handcuffs.

"My Muffie cracked the case?" Summer exclaimed. "My Muffie cracked the case!" Yeah. Summer was a little slow on the uptake. Not to mention off. Way off. Muffet helped for sure. But she was part of a case-cracking *team*.

"This is so exciting. Do you think we'll be in the paper?" Summer babbled.

Cassie looked at me and closed one eye really fast. It was that thing people do when they have a little secret, a little joke.

"It's no big deal," she said slyly. "Just a silly little hobby."

Ha, woof! This time, I totally got it.

CHAPTER 38

I pulled open the door to Pet Rescue, smiling at the sight of Bananas on Dodge's back. He'd practically galloped all the way from our house to make the ride special — it would be her last one for a good long while.

"Hey, team," Gwen greeted from behind the counter. Her smile was bright and her lap empty.

"Hi, Gwen! Where's Parsley?" I asked, hoping her lap cat was all right. We'd solved the case but some of Madame's cats had barely recovered.

"Right here," replied a voice. It was Erica Bloom, pushing through the door from the cat wing with Parsley, Cinnamon, and Trouble in her arms.

Gwen lifted a giant travel crate onto the counter. Erica carried the cats over, and together they jostled them inside.

"Reow!" Trouble complained.

"You're okay. We'll be home in a few minutes," Erica crooned to him. "And we'll have a yummy seafood dinner."

"Without shark liver oil, I hope," Gwen said, looking alarmed. "We just got all the cats healthy, and we want them to stay that way."

I nodded my agreement. "Too much vitamin A can cause a number of dangerous health issues in animals *and* humans."

Erica's dark eyes were solemn. "No shark, its liver, or its oil will cross their lips," she vowed, looking each of us in the eye. "And, oh! I wanted to ask you about garden fertilizer. . . ."

I looked at my feet while Erica questioned Gwen about the safety of garden fertilizer. I felt bad for ever suspecting that Erica had poisoned the cats. She'd actually been throwing out the fertilizer because she was afraid it might harm them. It was weird how much she complained about Madame LeFarge's cats, when deep down she actually cared about them — a lot.

"I just need you to initial and sign here," Gwen said, pointing to the adoption papers. "Then the cats are officially yours."

Erica signed with a flourish. "My little darlings!" she crowed, sounding a little like Madame herself. Gwen handed over her copy of the papers and Erica folded them and put them into her purse. "I'll see what I can do about Henry," she said. "I really think he could use a little company."

I blinked in surprise. "Henry? As in Henry Kales?"

Erica nodded. "Of course," she replied as she picked up her giant crate. "The poor man is terribly lonely. He could use a cat. And a little help with his social skills."

I shook my head as I watched Erica go. Who would've guessed? First she adopted three of the cats she'd complained about, and now she was going to convince Henry to adopt one as well? It didn't seem likely, but . . . I tapped my finger on my chin. You never knew. Dodge wasn't a cat lover (or even liker) until he met Bananas. Erica wasn't a cat lady until she had to live without them. So Henry . . . there might be hope for him, too.

I was still musing when I spotted a vaguely familiar blonde head walking toward the glass doors. Oh, no. Summer? Here? Now? I'd had enough of that girl to last for years. But it wasn't Summer — this blonde was older and taller.

The woman pulled open the door and walked gracefully up to the counter. "I'm interested in adopting a cat," she told Gwen. "My niece said you have several available right now."

I nodded, getting it. This was Summer's aunt. Which meant that Summer had kept her word. Which meant that . . .

I shook my head as Gwen dropped a couple of pizza crusts onto the floor for Dodge. I didn't want to think about what that meant. I quickly signed my own paperwork — for Bananas — and the three of us were on our way.

At Home Away, Paul and Esther were waiting with Duke in the front room.

"Hello, hello!" Duke said, getting up from his easy chair to give us hugs.

"Sit down!" Esther scolded. "The nurses said you're not one hundred percent yet."

Duke waved a hand. He still looked a little thin and pale, but his eyes were full of sparkle and he seemed much stronger than the last time I'd seen him.

"Dodge and I brought you a present," I told him, setting Bananas on his lap.

"A present?" Duke repeated, blinking. "For me?"

I nodded and winked at Paul and Esther. "Yes. Thanks to my friend Gwen's adoption magic, you've got a permanent visitor."

"Permanent?" Duke repeated. He lifted Bananas up and held her face close to his. "And what do you have to say about this, little one?"

"Meowf!" Bananas replied, starting to purr.

A giant smile spread across Duke's face, and he blinked even faster. "Well, it's settled, then."

Esther clapped her hands together. "How wonderful!"

"That's what we thought," I agreed. "Bananas here is very particular. But she loves Duke. And I'm pretty sure the feeling is mutual."

"I should say so," Paul agreed, reaching out a trembling hand to pet Bananas. Dodge stepped forward to nose Esther's purse, clearly on Peanut Butter Buddy patrol. Esther pulled out an entire package and unwrapped them all for Dodge.

I beamed happily at everyone while Dodge gobbled the treat — his second of the afternoon. Bananas was so busy purring at Duke that she didn't even notice. Duke rubbed her under the chin and whispered secrets in her pointy ears. They had it, too. Bananas and Duke. The same thing Dodge and I had. A bond. It totally confirmed my theory that there was a dog out there for every human. Except sometimes the dog wasn't exactly a dog — sometimes she just might be a cat.

a DOG and his GIRL MYSTERIES

DON'T MISS any of
Cassie and Dodge's adventures!